E.M'L

LOVE
IN
THE CLOUDS

Recent Books by Barbara Cartland

Barbara Cartland

LOVE
IN
THE CLOUDS

E.P. DUTTON
New York

For information contact: E.P. Dutton, 2 Park Avenue,
New York, N.Y. 10016

Library of Congress Cataloging in Publication Data:

Cartland, Barbara, 1902-
Love in the clouds.

I. Title.
PZ3.C247Lne 1979 [PS6005.A765] 823'.9'12 78-26007

ISBN: 0-525-14907-4

Published simultaneously in Canada by Clarke, Irwin
& Company Limited, Toronto and Vancouver

10 9 8 7 6 5 4 3 2 1

First Edition

AUTHOR'S NOTE

When I visited Nepal in 1958 I flew into the Happy Valley of Katmandu, but the difficult, dangerous road over the mountains to India was still in use. An easier one was opened the following year.

I loved this intriguing, beautiful little Eden and its attractive, smiling people, especially the Gurkhas. I stayed in one of the exquisite Palaces built by the family of the all powerful Prime Ministers, talked with the "Living Goddess," who was a little girl of six, and visited Monks from Tibet who blew for me their long brass trumpets.

It is impossible in Nepal—the Roof of the World—not to believe in the supernatural, in the legends with which the country abounds, and not to be aware that the breathtaking Himalayas hold spiritual secrets as yet unknown to the Western World.

The references to Sir Brian Hodgson and to Nana Sahib are all correct.

LOVE
IN
THE CLOUDS

Chapter One

1895

Coming back from the village, Chandra saw a chaise outside the front door and quickened her pace.

It was annoying that someone should have called to visit her father when she was not at home, and she knew that he did not want to be disturbed. However, she thought guiltily, it was her own fault, because if she had not stopped to gossip she would have arrived home twenty minutes earlier.

She always enjoyed going to the village because the owners of the small shops who had known her since she was a child were invariably ready to reminisce about the "old days" and her mother.

Mrs. Geary, in the baker's, invariably exclaimed as soon as she saw Chandra:

"Ah! There you are, Miss Wardell! And growing more like your dear mother every time I sees you."

"You could not say anything which would please me more," Chandra would reply.

Then Mrs. Geary would be off, telling long, rambling tales of how beautiful Chandra's mother had been when they first came to the Manor, and how everyone in the village had loved her.

This was true enough, Chandra thought, for her

1

mother had a gift for making friends wherever she went, and perhaps she used it more than another woman might have done, to make up for her husband's shortcomings.

Professor Barnard Wardell found people boring and wanted only to be left alone with his books.

He was the greatest Sanskrit scholar of his day. The Royal Asiatic Society had made him a Member, he was a Fellow of the Royal Society, and the Société Asiatique de Paris paid him high distinction.

Unfortunately, the general public was not interested in his works of scholarship, which meant, of course, that his books were not widely saleable.

He received a grant—a very small one—from the Asiatic Society of Bengal, but otherwise they had to rely on a small amount of royalties which arrived intermittently from his publishers.

"Do you not think, Papa," Chandra had said to him dozens of times, "that you could write a book that would interest ordinary people who would like to know more about the East and the literary treasures that they do not even know exist?"

"I am not throwing my pearls of wisdom before swine!" her father had replied.

"But, Papa, we need money, and careful though I am with every penny you give me, we cannot exist on air."

She knew, even as she spoke, that her father was not listening to her.

His mind was far away in a Lamasery in Tibet or a Monastery in the foothills of the Himalayas, anywhere where the sages of the past had hidden their manuscripts, which none other than scholarly men could decipher.

Sometimes when she read of the sales of a popular novel or a travel-book running into thousands of copies, Chandra would wish her father were different.

Then she knew proudly that he was unique and

that whatever the difficulties she would not have him change.

It was because they were so short of money and it was quite impossible for the Professor to afford a secretary or an assistant that five years ago Chandra had started working with him on his translations.

After the initial work, which was very exhausting, she found it interesting and in fact absorbing.

However, the Professor was not a good teacher. He was impatient and given to shouting at his daughter when she found it hard to understand some very difficult Sanskrit word or an almost incomprehensible nuance of grammar.

But gradually, as the years passed, because she was extremely intelligent Chandra grew more and more proficient, until in this last twelve months she found herself doing most of the draft translation of a manuscript, leaving her father the easier job of revising.

He was getting older, and the long journeys he had taken to obscure parts of the world, where he had contracted malaria and every other sort of Asiatic fever, were now beginning to take their toll.

But he would never admit to weakness, so Chandra would say to him:

"I will finish this, Papa. There is a very interesting article in today's newspaper on which I would like you to give me your opinion. I have put it by your chair."

Her father would obey her and sit down in his favourite chair, only to fall asleep almost as soon as he had picked up the newspaper, which was, Chandra thought, proof of the fact that while he would not admit to his fatigue, it was nevertheless undeniable.

She thought now, as she hurried down the short drive, which was badly in need of weeding because they could not afford a gardener, that it would not only annoy her father to have a visitor but would undoubtedly tire him.

She had had a suspicion recently that he was forcing himself to use up his strength and do more than was really prudent.

Chandra reached the open chaise and saw that it was drawn by two horses and on the box there was a very smart groom wearing a cockaded hat.

She wondered who could be the caller, knowing from the style of the conveyance in which he had come that it was certainly not one of her father's literary friends, who were mostly as impoverished as he was.

She only hoped that it was not Lady Dorritt from the Castle, because if there was one person whom her father really detested, it was the Lord Lieutenant's wife, who was not only infuriatingly patronising but also extremely garrulous.

Yet Chandra had never known Lady Dorritt to drive in anything but a closed carriage, and therefore, even though it was warm for September, she was unlikely to be her father's visitor.

She waked into the oak-panelled hall, where a beautifully carved Elizabethan staircase curved up to the first floor.

It was as she was hurrying towards the Study, where she knew her father would be ensconced with his visitor, that she saw on an oak chair a man's tall hat.

She then knew that whoever was with her father, it was not Lady Dorritt, although it did not suggest the identity of the caller.

Chandra's hand was actually outstretched towards the door of the Study when she heard a deep voice which she did not recognise, and she stood listening.

She could not hear very clearly what was being said, so on an impulse, instead of entering the room she moved quickly to another door in the hall, opened it, and entered the Drawing-Room.

This was a room that was seldom used since her

mother's death and the curtains were drawn to prevent the sunshine from fading the carpet, because
the fewer rooms that were used, the easier it was for
old Ellen, who was the only person left, to serve
them.

Moving silently across the carpet, Chandra went to
a corner of the room where there was a corner-cabinet
let into the wall, probably in Queen Anne's time when
the room had first been panelled.

It was, however, only recently that Chandra had
discovered that when she opened the door of the cupboard, in which were arranged various attractive
pieces of china, she could hear distinctly what was
said in the Study next door.

She imagined that in order to fit the cupboard, the
bricks had been removed until only a thin veneer of
plaster had been left on the wall in the next room.

When she told her father of her discovery he had
laughed.

"I cannot believe that this house, which belonged
to a most respectable County family until my father
bought it, was ever used for spying. Nevertheless, we
might find your secret listening-post convenient."

"How, Papa?" Chandra asked.

"When some of those bores who call stay too long,"
her father replied, "I will merely raise my voice a
little and you can come and rescue me."

"There is no need to raise your voice, Papa," Chandra replied. "We will just have a code. If you say:
'It is cold for this time of the year,' I shall know you
are anxious to be rid of them, but if you say: 'I smell
smoke,' I shall know that you need rescuing immediately."

"I always need that whenever you inflict those chat-
tering fools on me," her father growled. "Why I cannot be left alone I cannot imagine!"

It was a constant cry of the Professor's, for all he
wanted was to be alone with his books; and as he

made this very obvious to anyone who called on him, he was in fact frequently undisturbed for weeks on end.

As Chandra now pulled open the cupboard door, she heard the deep voice that she had listened to in the hall, saying:

"If my information is correct, it will be the most amazing find of all time!"

"I agree with you," the Professor replied, "but you know as well as I do that reports of such manuscripts are usually based on hearsay, and they generally turn out to be entirely valueless."

"My informant is a man of complete integrity, but of course he may have been mistaken."

"Has he been of actual help to you in the past?"

"I have always found him very reliable, and he took the trouble to come all the way to Calcutta to see me, just as I was boarding my ship to return to England."

"It certainly sounds as though he was convinced, but you have not told me yet, Lord Frome, how I can help you."

Chandra started.

She knew now who her father's visitor was.

Damon Frome was one of the younger men interested in Sanskrit treasures and her father had often mentioned him.

The Professor had in fact been sent several manuscripts by Damon Frome in the past two years, which Chandra had helped him to translate.

They had, she remembered now, been much more exciting and much older than most of the other papers on which her father had worked.

What was more, he had been better paid for the time he had spent on them.

If Lord Frome had brought her father some new work, she thought with delight, that was exactly what they needed at the moment.

Just before she had left the village, Mr. Dart, the grocer, had said to her:

"I knows the Professor's busy, Miss Chandra, but if yer could ask him if he'd give us a little on account, I'd be most grateful."

Mr. Dart was a nervous, somewhat inarticulate man, not the type of blustering, exuberant character one would expect in his trade.

Chandra knew he had keyed himself up to speak to her and she was uncomfortably conscious that their bill with Mr. Dart had been growing higher and higher for several months.

"I will speak to Papa, Mr. Dart," she said quickly. "I am sure he must have overlooked what we owe you. You know how absent-minded he is."

"I apologise for troubling you, Miss Chandra, and the Professor," Mr. Dart replied, "but times are hard, and it's difficult to order from my wholesaler without paying cash."

"I understand, Mr. Dart," Chandra said, "and I will speak to my father as soon as I reach home."

To relieve the discomfort of the situation, she had asked after Mrs. Dart and the children, all of whom she knew by name.

Yet as she walked away from the small shop with its bow-fronted window, she wondered how it would be possible to let Mr. Dart have even a token payment of what he was owed.

She could, of course, write to her father's publishers. She had done that in the past, and he had been very angry when he had found out that she had done so.

But there was very little chance of their agreeing to let her have any further payment on the books that they had published the previous year, which, though praised in the scholarly reviews, aroused no response from the public.

'I wonder if there is anything left in the house to

sell?' Chandra had thought as she walked back along the country lane.

She had known the answer even as she asked the question.

Now she felt her spirits rise.

Lord Frome had brought her father some work and she was confident that everything would now, and in the future, be different.

"What I want in this instance," Lord Frome was saying, "is your help, Professor, in a different way from anything we have done together before."

"A different way?" her father asked in a puzzled tone.

"In the past," Lord Frome said, "I have brought to you manuscripts I have discovered in Tibet and the Himalayas, and you have translated them for me with an expertise which, if I may say so, is unrivalled anywhere in the Western World."

"That is very kind of you," Chandra heard her father say, and she knew how much he enjoyed the compliment.

"But as this manuscript is so precious, so different from anything I have found before," Lord Frome went on, "I not only want you to translate it for me, but first to help me find it."

"Find it?" the Professor echoed.

"To be quite frank," Lord Frome said, "I am not certain that I would recognise it if I saw it."

There was silence for a moment, and Chandra was sure that her father was looking at Lord Frome with a perplexed expression on his face.

"What I mean, Professor," Lord Frome said, as if in answer to an unvoiced question, "is that you should come with me to Nepal."

"Do you think that is where the manuscript is to be found?" Professor Wardell asked.

"My informant tells me that it is in a Lamasery in the mountains beyond Katmandu. He is almost certain that the Abbot and the Monks have no idea of the value of what they have in their possession. In fact, he thinks they are not men of great learning but of a deep piety."

"That, of course, should make the acquisition of it easier," the Professor said in a practical manner.

"That is what I thought," Lord Frome agreed. "At the same time, I am told that there are hundreds if not thousands of manuscripts in this Lamasery, and unless I intend to spend a number of years there searching through them, I must have your help."

"You are really asking me to go with you to Nepal? I have heard that it is very difficult to enter that country."

"It is," Lord Frome agreed. "In fact, few Europeans have been permitted access, with the exception of the British Resident."

"Of course," the Professor said. "Sir Brian Hodgson was the British Resident until, I think, 1843."

"Correct!" Lord Frome said. "But then, unfortunately, owing to the bungling of Lord Ellenborough, he resigned and afterwards, as you know, became something of a recluse in Darjeeling, where he did the most amazing work on Sanskrit manuscripts."

"Of course, of course!" the Professor said. "I have seen most of those that he presented to the Royal Asiatic Society and the India Office Library."

"So have I," Lord Frome said; "both are fantastic collections and posterity should be extremely grateful."

"I doubt that!" the Professor murmured, but Lord Frome went on:

"There is a British Resident in Nepal at the moment. Fortunately, he has persuaded the Prime Minister to give permission for me and an assistant to enter the country. We are not supposed to stay long, but I understand that once we are in, it may be possible to extend our time limit."

"You make it sound easier than I expected," the Professor remarked.

"Nothing is easy when you are dealing with the Orient," Lord Frome replied. "We shall just have to take things step by step. The first stage is that we have permission to visit Nepal for a limited time."

"The Nepalese will not make difficulties about removing one of their treasures?" the Professor questioned.

"I doubt if they know the value of them, not of course in terms of money, but in intellectual importance," Lord Frome answered. "I do not need to tell you, Professor, that if we find, as I hope we shall, the Lotus Manuscript as you and I call it, the whole thinking world will ultimately benefit."

"We can but pray," the Professor said, "that your informant has not been beguiled by false information."

"I have a hunch, and I follow my hunches," Lord Frome said, "that we will find what we seek and somehow we will bring it back here so that you can work on it."

Her father's visitor must have risen as he spoke, for Chandra heard a chair scraped back. Then Lord Frome said:

"I am leaving tonight, but I hope you will be able to join me as quickly as possible at Bairagnia."

"How shall I do that?" Professor Wardell enquired.

"I took the liberty," Lord Frome replied, "because of the urgency of my quest, of booking a cabin for you on the P. & O. Liner *Bezwada,* which will be leaving Southampton next Wednesday. By the time you reach Bombay I shall have already set off for the North, but I will wait for you at Bairagnia."

There was a slight pause, and Chandra felt that Lord Frome was smiling as he said:

"I know you have done a lot of riding in the past, Professor, and I hope you have not neglected such exercise while you have been living here in England."

"You are saying it will need hard riding to enter Nepal?" the Professor asked.

"The railway ends at Bairagnia, and after that there will be at least two days over rough, mountainous country before the road, if you can give it such a pretentious name, drops down into Katmandu."

"It cannot be worse than the ride I took into Tibet ten years ago," the Professor remarked. "I often wonder why I was not frozen to death on the passes or lost in the snow-storms which made it almost impossible to find the path after they were over."

Lord Frome laughed.

"One unwary step and you find yourself hurtling down a precipice! Nepal is not as bad as that, although it is called the Roof of the World."

"You reassure me, My Lord," the Professor said drily.

"Here is your ticket for the boat," Lord Frome went on, "and enough money for your expenses on the voyage. One of my servants will, of course, meet you at Bombay, and he will have all the reservations already made for you on the train. He will travel with you and look after you, I am certain, to your satisfaction."

"I have always heard," the Professor said, "that you are a very efficient traveller, My Lord."

"I am," Lord Frome replied with some hardness in his voice. "I make my plans well ahead, and if they are not disrupted and the unforeseeable does not happen, everything goes smoothly! Or else I want to know the reason why!"

"I shall look forward to our collaboration in Nepal," the Professor answered. "I can only hope that as you are always so extremely successful, My Lord, you will not on this occasion be disappointed."

"I very much doubt it," Lord Frome replied.

Chandra could hear the two men moving across the

room. Then they were in the hall and she knew her father was escorting Lord Frome to the front door.

She thought of joining them, then decided against it.

She had the feeling, although she was not quite certain why, that Lord Frome would not be interested in meeting her or in knowing any details of her father's private life.

He had certainly shown no awareness that he might be disrupting the Professor's family, if he had one, by his peremptory demands that he leave almost immediately for Nepal.

There had been, Chandra thought, something authoritative and determined about Lord Frome's voice, which she resented.

He was obviously a man who was used to having his own way; a man who gave orders without even contemplating that they might be disregarded.

He wanted her father and had assumed that he would be willing to do exactly what he wished.

Of course he had known that the Professor would be thrilled to hear about a unique manuscript hitherto unknown. But, Chandra thought resentfully, he might have shown a little more humanity.

He might have apologised for the inconvenience and the nervous strain he would be causing an elderly man by expecting him to leave his home in England at a few days' notice.

"He just expects Papa to be at his beck and call," she told herself.

As she heard the front door close, she joined her father from the darkened Drawing-Room.

He was walking back into his Study with what she thought was an almost dazed expression on his face.

"Papa . . ." she began, only to be interrupted as the Professor said:

"Did you overhear what was said, Chandra? I thought you might be next door."

"Yes, Papa. I was listening."

"Just think of it—the Lotus Manuscript! It is something which I have heard and dreamt about ever since I was a boy. I never thought I would see it—actually hold it in my hands!"

"You cannot be certain you will find that particular manuscript, Papa, but please tell me about it. I do not seem to remember hearing you speak of it before."

The Professor threw himself down in a leather-covered armchair, that was faded and worn but was still the most comfortable chair in the room.

"The Lotus Manuscript," he said, "which is the colloquial name for it amongst those who study Oriental writings, is supposed to have been written by one of Buddha's disciples when he was still alive. It records sayings of Buddha which do not appear in any other books. Because it was so sacred to his followers, it was hidden soon after his death in case it should ever get into the wrong hands."

"Where was it hidden?" Chandra enquired.

Her father made an expressive gesture with his hands.

"It was, I understand, taken from one Lamasery to another, carried over mountains and across rivers, but always treated with great reverence, and yet never resting anywhere for long."

Chandra knew from her studies of the East that this was typical of those who always suspected that there might be thieves to steal what was so precious, or, worse still, enemies who would wish to destroy what they did not understand.

"Do you really think that anything so valuable could end up in an unimportant Lamasery in Nepal?"

"We know from the Hodgson Collection how unexpectedly important the Buddhist Sanskrit works in Nepal have proved to be," the Professor replied. "There is no reason why this Lamasery, which now may not be of very great importance, should not have had, in the past, an Abbot who was trusted by those who were trying to save the Lotus Manuscript."

"No, of course, I understand," Chandra said. "But, Papa, you do realise that this will be a very arduous trip? Do you really think you will be well enough to undertake it? And especially to ride over the mountains?"

Her father did not answer and she went on:

"I know you have done it in the past. You have told me so much about your travels, but, Papa, you were much . . . younger then."

"I am not yet in my dotage," the Professor answered sharply, "and I see no reason why you should imagine I cannot undertake the type of journey I have done a dozen times in the past."

Chandra was about to say: "Because you are so much older," then bit back the words.

She knew by her father's face that he was enraptured by the idea of what to him would be a voyage of discovery, and there was no use trying to persuade him not to do what he wanted. Instead, the kindest part she could play would be to help him and see to his comfort in every way she could.

She moved towards him and kissed him lightly on the forehead.

"It is very exciting for you, Papa," she said, "and I only wish I could go with you."

"I wish you could too, my dear," the Professor replied, "and quite frankly I shall miss you."

Chandra knew that this was true.

He would miss her not only because she had attended to him personally but also because he had grown to rely on her in their work together.

"I am sure you will manage quite well without me," she said aloud, to give him confidence. "There is only one difficulty . . . what am I to live on while you are away?"

She quite expected her father to say he could not

be bothered by such trivialities, but instead he replied:

"You obviously did not hear what Lord Frome told me after we had left the Study."

"What was that, Papa?"

"He said: 'I forgot to mention, Professor, that of course I insist on paying for your services. Here is a cheque for six hundred pounds, and there will be another six hundred for you when you return home with the manuscript to work on.' "

Chandra drew in her breath.

"Twelve hundred pounds, Papa! I can hardly believe it!"

"It sounds like a lot," her father replied. "At the same time, there will be expenses, and of course we do not know how long it will take me to translate the manuscript."

For a moment Chandra was prepared to dismiss this as unimportant.

What mattered was that she could pay the outstanding bills in the village and also that she and Ellen could exist without starving while her father was away.

Because she was so pleased she flung her arms round his neck, kissed him excitedly, and said:

"This is marvellous, Papa! Really marvellous! I was just wondering as I came home from the village how I could tell you that Mr. Dart had asked for us to pay him something on his long-outstanding account."

"Now you can pay the lot!" the Professor said. "And all the other trades-people to whom we may owe anything."

"We owe a good deal," Chandra said with a smile, knowing how absent-minded her father was about such things. "But everything will be all right now. Oh, Papa, I must go and tell Ellen!"

As she spoke, she ran off to the small kitchen, where Ellen, who had been her mother's maid but now looked after Chandra and the Professor since her death, was preparing tea.

She was cutting wafer-thin cucumber sandwiches, which were her father's favourite, and Chandra knew by the expression on her face that she was worrying as she always did about their household problems.

"Ellen, what do you think?" she cried as she entered the kitchen.

"What do I think, Miss Chandra?" Ellen replied, looking up. "I think you are late for tea, that's what I think. And there's a visitor."

"The visitor has gone, Ellen," Chandra replied. "And hold your breath, because you will not believe it, but he has left behind him a cheque for six hundred pounds!"

"Now, Miss Chandra, I want none of your jokes. Money, when you haven't any, is no laughing matter."

"I am not joking, but I am laughing, for it is true, Ellen! Lord Frome, Papa's visitor, has left a cheque for six hundred pounds to pay Papa to go out to Nepal with him."

Ellen put down the bread-knife and stared at Chandra as if she had taken leave of her senses. Then she said:

"Going out to Nepal? That's impossible, Miss Chandra, as well you know!"

"No, it is true, Ellen. Papa has agreed to go. In fact, he is longing to. Do you think it will be too much for him?"

"It's not only too much, Miss Chandra, it'll be the death of the Master—that's what it'll be!"

Chandra did not reply and Ellen went on:

"Your mother said to me often enough in the past that those long journeys into outlandish places would kill him before he's finished. And how do you think he can go gallivanting at his time of life?"

Chandra looked stricken.

"I did think it might prove too much for him, El-

len, but he is so thrilled by the idea and quite determined to go. And think of it—now we can pay all our
debts! Mr. Dart asked me only this afternoon if we
could pay something on account. I told him I would
speak to Papa, but I knew there was little hope of set-
tling his bill."

"Money's not everything, Miss Chandra!" Ellen
said with a sniff, cutting another piece of bread almost
fiercely. "Your father's a sick man, although he won't
admit it."

Chandra sat down on a chair by the table.

"If he does not go, then we shall have to give this
money back to Lord Frome. How then are we going
to live?"

"I don't know, Miss Chandra, and that's a fact,"
Ellen said. "I know your father's not well enough to
go climbing mountains and such-like, and your mother
always said those fevers which left him as weak as a
baby did no good to his heart."

"You are frightening me, Ellen."

"Somebody has to have a head on their shoulders in
this household," Ellen replied.

She arranged the cucumber sandwiches neatly on a
plate and took up the tray, on which she had already
set a lace-edged cloth and a pretty china tea-set.

The silver which they had used in her mother's day
had been sold long ago.

Ellen always made her father's tea in exactly the
same way as he had had it when her mother was alive.

Chandra often wondered if he noticed how daintily
served everything was and if he would have worried
if it had been otherwise.

Carrying the tray, Ellen walked ahead down the
passage and Chandra followed her.

Only as she reached the hall did she hurry forward
to open the door into the Study so that Ellen could
carry in the tray without having to put it down.

Her father was sitting where she had left him, in

the leather-covered arm-chair, and there was a smile on his lips which told Chandra how happy he was about everything.

"Your tea, Sir," Ellen said, setting it down on a table beside him.

"Thank you, Ellen. I expect Miss Chandra has told you the exciting news?"

"It sounds exciting, Sir," Ellen replied, "but have you thought of how much it'll tax your strength?"

"I have been thinking that it will be quite one of the most exciting journeys I have ever undertaken in my life," the Professor said with satisfaction.

"I was just calculating, Sir," Ellen went on, as if he had not spoken, "that it's nearly ten years since you last went on a journey of this sort. Then, if you recall, it was to Sikkim."

"Ah, yes, I remember it well!" the Professor said. "It was a very interesting trip, but not quite so rewarding as I had hoped."

He looked up at Chandra and said:

"You will remember I brought back some small Buddhist works which are now in the India Office Library, but they were not as old as we had hoped for."

"When I read them a few years ago, Papa, they were not early enough to be of real value," Chandra answered, "at least from a collector's point of view."

"That was ten years ago, Sir," Ellen persisted.

"All right, Ellen, ten years ago!" the Professor agreed. "But I am still young enough to go to Nepal."

"I hope you will think so when you get there, Sir," Ellen said tartly, and as if she could not continue to speak without saying things for which she later might be sorry, she flounced from the room.

The Professor smiled.

"Ellen has always wanted to mollycoddle me, just as your mother used to do. Now you, my dear, are far more sensible. You realise that this literally is the opportunity of a lifetime and nothing would make me miss it."

"No, I understand," Chandra answered, "and I admit to being very excited myself about the Lotus Manuscript."

"You will be able to help me translate it," the Professor said, "and perhaps this will be the one piece of Sanskrit which will really capture the mind of the modern world."

"That would indeed be a miracle," Chandra said bitterly.

She knew how little interest was shown in the works her father had already translated, which to her were full of beautiful, inspiring thoughts, which could stimulate and raise towards the stars the minds of those who understood them.

She knew that where she was concerned, her father's work, which was often dismissed as "dusty old books," had opened new horizons and brought her an awareness of great spiritual teachings.

Her father now put out his hand and took hers as she stood beside him.

"You have been a good daughter to me, Chandra, since your mother died," he said. "I miss her, I miss her more every day, but I have had you and that has helped a great deal."

"I am glad about that, Papa," Chandra replied, "and whatever Ellen may say, of course you must go on this journey. You will feel like Jason looking for the Golden Fleece, and even if the manuscript is not there when you arrive, there will be the excitement of the search."

Her father nodded his head and she thought as she looked at him that there was a new light in his eyes and he looked younger than he had before.

'It is hope that matters when one is getting old,' she thought to herself, 'in fact hope at any time of

life. It is a far better tonic than any Doctor can provide out of a bottle.'

She pressed her father's hand and said:

"I am going upstairs to the attic now, Papa, to find
all the things Mama and I packed away when you
came back from your journey to Sikkim. We put lots
of moth-balls with them, so there is no reason why they
should not be just as good as when you last wore them.
What is more, you have not put on weight, so they
should fit you perfectly."

Her father laughed and patted his stomach.

"No, I still have a flat tummy, and it will not be
hard for a horse to carry me up the mountains."

"I shall expect you to keep a diary of everything
that happens from day to day," Chandra said, "so that
I can read it when you come home and feel, even
though I have been left behind, that I have travelled
with you."

"It is not a journey fit for a woman," her father
said, as if he had been half-wishing that she could accompany him.

"You did not say that when Mama insisted on going with you to Sikkim," Chandra replied. "And do
not forget, Papa, that I went with you to India when
it was so hot that summer on the Plains."

"You were," the Professor replied, "a very good
traveller, even at a young age."

Chandra paused as she opened the door.

"I suppose, Papa," she said in a rather small voice,
"that there is no point in asking Lord Frome if I could
come with you? After all, anyone as important as you
is entitled to an assistant, or if you like I could be your
valet."

The Professor laughed.

"I have managed without a valet all my life, but I
would certainly like to take you as my assistant! It
would, however, be a waste of time to ask Frome, of
all people."

"Why of all people?" Chandra asked curiously.

"Because he has a reputation for being a woman-hater," the Professor replied. "I have heard all sorts of stories about it one way or another. They all say he started travelling round the world in the first place because he had a broken heart."

Chandra came back into the room.

"How fascinating!" she said. "Do you know who broke it?"

"I have not the slightest idea," the Professor replied. "All I know is that Frome is very much a man's man. Proud, abrupt, and seldom troubles to make himself charming to anybody, least of all to women."

"How long have you known him, Papa?"

"Oh, a number of years," the Professor replied, "and our paths have crossed on several occasions. I remember meeting him in India when your mother was with me. She never liked him."

Chandra sat down in the chair opposite her father.

"Why did Mama not like him?"

"She thought him a rather domineering, aggressive young man, which he certainly was in those days."

"And now?"

"He has no need to be aggressive, but he is domineering just by being himself."

It was Chandra's turn to laugh.

"You are describing him very eloquently, Papa. Go on!"

"I really do not know what else to tell you," he said. "He came into the title when he was quite young, but he does not use it. He prefers to call himself Damon Frome unless he wants to pull strings to get his own way. That, I imagine, is what he has done on this occasion, to get into Nepal."

"But why is he particularly interested in Sanskrit?"

The Professor shrugged his shoulders.

"I have no idea! It certainly seems a strange interest for a young man, but he undoubtedly has collected a number of extremely valuable manuscripts in the past, mostly from Tibet, and as you know, over the years he has sent me quite a number to translate."

"When they have been translated, what does he do with them?"

"He publishes them, and I get a certain amount of royalties from the books if they sell, which they do not in any appreciable number."

"I think he sounds rather mysterious," Chandra said. "How old is he, Papa?"

The Professor gave a shrug of his shoulders.

"Thirty-three — thirty-four — thirty-five — I really have no idea," he said. "He is one of those men who might be any age. I can only estimate that he must still be young, because he was only a mere boy when we first met."

"But he is rich?"

"Very rich, I believe. Most such men of his age are enjoying themselves in London, as Members of the 'Marlborough House Set,' racing at Newmarket, trying to win the Derby, grouse-shooting in Scotland, or yachting at Cowes."

Chandra clapped her hands.

"Oh, Papa! You are such fun! You always behave as if your head is in the clouds, but when it comes down to brass-tacks you know a great deal more than your pretend to about the Social World."

"A world in which I have no interest and which I have never been able to afford," the Professor replied. "Your mother would have enjoyed it when we were young, although I do not think she really missed it."

"Mama missed nothing when she was with you," Chandra said. "If you had asked her to live on the moon, she would have made the best of it and I suspect would have made it quite comfortable."

"That is true," the Professor agreed. "Although we suffered a great deal of discomfort one way or another, we always managed to laugh at life because we just liked being together."

"I was there too," Chandra reminded him in a small voice.

"I know, my dearest, and we thought you were the most entrancing child any two people could have, even though we were disappointed at having only one. But I doubt if we could have afforded any more."

"You certainly could not have taken more than one over deserts, across India, and all those other strange places we visited," Chandra said.

The Professor gave a sigh.

"I am always glad that your mother had her last years here. She always longed to have a home."

"She made it a very happy one," Chandra said. "Even now when I come into the house I expect to hear her voice saying: 'Is that you, darling?'"

She saw a sudden mist over her father's eyes and wished she had not spoken.

Then, as if it suddenly struck him, he asked:

"You will be all right while I am gone?"

"Ellen will be with me."

"I hope I will not be too long."

"I hope so too, Papa. I shall miss you, so you had better give me plenty of work to do."

"There is still quite a lot left undone of the latest manuscripts from the Royal Asiatic Society," the Professor remarked.

"Yes, of course," Chandra agreed, "so I will get down to them. But it will not be the same, Papa, as working with you."

The Professor rose to his feet.

"If it was anyone else but Frome," he said, "I would damn the consequences and say you had to come with me, but he is such an unpredictable man. I believe his reply would be that he would get somebody else."

"And that would break your heart, Papa, you know

it would!" Chandra exclaimed. "Never mind, I will follow you in my thoughts, and I shall pray every day that you really will find the Lotus Manuscript and bring it back for me to see."

"Then with another six · hundred pounds in our pockets we will celebrate," the Professor said, "and you shall have everything you want. That I promise you!"

Chandra rose from the seat and put her arms round her father to kiss him once again.

"You will take care of yourself, Papa, will you not?" she pleaded. "I will be very uneasy, with Ellen worrying about you all the time."

"If Ellen had her way I would be in a wheel-chair! All women, whatever their age, like an invalid so that they can bully him!"

Chandra laughed, then said:

"Now I am going to the attic, and I do not mind betting you, Papa, that I shall find Ellen there already. You know that whatever she says aloud, in her heart she is very proud of your achievements, just as I am."

"That is what your mother used to say," the Professor replied. "And I would so much like to find the Lotus Manuscript, if only because she would have been so pleased."

"If you do find it, Papa, I shall believe it is because she has helped you to do so," Chandra answered.

Now she walked resolutely towards the door, knowing that though it was fascinating to stay talking to her father, there was a great deal for her to do.

As she walked up the stairs she thought wistfully of the fun it would be if only she could go with him as she had on their trips in the past.

Looking back, she thought they had always seemed filled with laughter, even when there were catastrophes, like the time one of their mules, carrying a lot of precious possessions, had fallen over a precipice to be lost in the valley below.

It had all been part of an adventure, just as when they were becalmed for days on end in a small ship travelling in the Red Sea and they had run out of water.

Chandra could look back on innumerable instances which might have made another person cry, but her mother had always managed to smile.

"It might be worse," she would say. "After all, we are all alive and well, and so far the mast has not broken on our heads and no crocodile has eaten us!"

It was her mother who made her father comfortable in the most impossible places. It was her mother who seemed somehow to provide food when they were tired and inclined to be disagreeable. Her mother had surrounded her father with an aura of love which made it impossible, however poor they were, to be anything but happy.

'Papa always had Mama to look after him,' Chandra thought, 'and since she died, Ellen and I have done our best! I do not really believe he could manage without us.'

She had an uncomfortable conviction that this was the truth. Then she asked herself what she could do about it.

It would not only make her father happy to go on this journey to Nepal, it would also settle the immediate problem of their financial difficulties. There was no money left in the bank with which they could purchase even the merest necessities of life.

"It is just providential that it has happened at this moment," Chandra told herself.

She took off the small hat she had been wearing and, walking into her bedroom, laid it down on a chair.

It was still too hot to need a coat, and she thought that her gown, which was faded from many washings and pressings, was in fact very shabby.

Perhaps it was a good thing that she had not gone

into the Study to speak to Lord Frome, even though she would have liked to meet him.

He might have thought that he would get the Professor more cheaply because it was obvious that his daughter was badly in need of a new dress.

Then she told herself that she was attributing quite unfair qualities to the man she should be looking on as a benefactor.

After all, he had been very generous in his treatment of her father and had certainly anticipated that he would need money on the train journey across India.

That, at any rate, was sensible, Chandra told herself a little grudgingly, then smiled because she knew that she was resenting Lord Frome simply because he was the type of man of whom her father could not ask a favour.

"He is taking Papa away from me and I think really I hate him for that!" she told her reflection in the mirror.

Then, because she sounded so serious, she smiled.

"A woman-hater!" she said aloud. "If only he were not one, it might have made all the difference to my life!"

Chapter Two

Chandra came downstairs carrying yet more things to add to the large pile of luggage already assembled in the hall.

She had always thought it was easy to travel light, but now she had found instead that her father required so many things that she had already teased him by saying he would need a special elephant to carry them.

A number of them were, of course, essential to his work, and he would have been lost without them, just as he would not have thought of going off anywhere without a number of books that he wished to read.

He was determined to know a great deal about Nepal before he reached it.

It was one of the few places in the East which he had not visited in the past, and he and Chandra found they were absorbed by what they could learn from the numerous books which filled the Study walls from floor to ceiling.

The majority of course were out-of-date, but there were a number relating to the past history of the Monarchy of Nepal. They learnt that since 1857 power had rested with the Prime Minister, while the King was only the symbolic head of the country.

It all sounded fascinating, but as far as Chandra was concerned there were so many other things to be done that she could only glance at her father's books and listen to what he told her in the evenings when the work was done.

Now that he was leaving, she found herself thinking continually of Ellen's anxiety about him, and although the old maid said very little, Chandra was aware that she thought it unlikely her father would survive the journey.

Sometimes in the darkness Chandra would find herself talking to her mother and asking her advice.

"What am I to do, Mama?" she would ask. "You know how much Papa is looking forward to finding the Lotus Manuscript, and also we need the money. We need it desperately, and it is really a gift from the gods that Lord Frome should have turned up at this exact moment."

She felt that her mother understood, and yet the worrying doubt as to whether she was doing the right thing in letting her father leave was always with her.

Not, she told herself, that she would have been able to stop him. There was only one person who had ever been able to alter her father's mind once he had made it up, and that had been her mother.

"He will go if it kills him!" she told herself over and over again.

Then she thought that perhaps if such a tragedy did happen, it would be the way her father would want to die.

Today the last things that Ellen and she felt necessary for her father's comfort had been cleaned, his clothes washed and pressed, and as Chandra added what she carried in her hands, she thought that that really must be enough.

Tomorrow they would have one more day together

and she wanted to spend every moment of it in her father's company, before they would have to leave very early next morning to reach Southampton.

Chandra was determined to go with him and see him on board and make his cabin as comfortable as possible.

'I will take some roses with me,' she thought, 'and they will remind him of home as he passes through the Bay of Biscay, which is certain to be rough.'

She walked across the hall and into the Study, where, as she expected, her father was at his desk working.

"What are you doing now, Papa?" she asked.

"I am just polishing up my knowledge of the Nepalese language," he said.

"It is different from Urdu?" Chandra enquired.

"The Newari language is related to the Tibetan and Burmese," the Professor replied, "and retains a mono-syllabic character. It does not have a script of its own but has adopted Sanskrit and modified it to its own needs."

"I think I did know that," Chandra replied. "But will you find it difficult to understand Newari?"

"I hope not," her father replied. "As you know, I speak so many different languages and dialects that I expect I shall make myself understood."

Chandra leant over his shoulder and looked at the words he was writing down and realised that he was translating the more ordinary sentences which he would require.

She made her father pronounce one or two of them to her, then repeated them after him.

"It is not too difficult for us because we can read Sanskrit," he said, "but I imagine that a complete foreigner to the country would find it extremely hard."

Chandra gave a little sigh.

"Oh, Papa, I do wish I were coming with you!

There are so many things we could do together which would be amusing."

Her father sighed too.

"I know, my dearest, but I assure you that Lord Frome would be horrified at such an idea! I am sure he would take somebody else and want his money back."

Chandra held up her hands in horror.

"Do not suggest such a thing! The whole village is celebrating because we have paid our debts! They have not felt so affluent for years!"

"It is lucky that I have not had to buy new equipment," the Professor said, "so I shall not have to worry about you and Ellen not having enough money while I am away."

"You are the one we have to worry about."

Chandra put her arm round his shoulders and said:

"Stop working, Papa; I want you to spend every moment until tomorrow with me. Why do we not walk in the garden? It is a lovely, warm day and the air will do you good."

"Very well, my dear," the Professor agreed. "I will just put these books back on the shelf so that I can find them when next I want them."

"I will help you," Chandra said.

She picked up a number of books which her father had thrown carelessly on the floor and carried them across the room.

She tried to arrange the volumes he used frequently in some sort of order so that they would not waste time in looking for a book when they wanted it.

But there were so many, and they covered such a wide range of different countries and subjects, that however hard she tried, she usually found that the book she wanted quickly was one which had been moved to some inaccessible spot.

Chandra put those she carried in her arms tidily in place, then turned to see that her father was climbing the step-ladder to place on one of the top shelves some books he had been reading.

"Let me do that, Papa," she said.

But he was already standing on the top of the steps, slipping the books into place.

Only as he put the last one in did he murmur something which Chandra could not hear, and as she looked at him questioningly he seemed to sway.

"Papa!" she exclaimed, but even as she spoke she realised that he was falling.

He clutched at the side of the bookcase, then as his feet seemed to slip he half-fell, half-slithered from the steps to the floor.

He pulled Chandra down with him, and she undoubtedly prevented his fall from being as hard as it might have been.

"Oh, Papa!" she said again, and realised that with his eyes shut he was breathing laboriously, while his hand had gone to his heart.

She knew what had happened and that the Doctor's forebodings had come true. Her father had had a heart-attack.

With difficulty she moved him into a more comfortable position, reaching behind her for a cushion from the chair to put under his head.

Then, rising to her feet, she ran to the door, opened it, and shouted:

"Ellen! Ellen!"

Her voice seemed to ring out round the small house and the old maid came hurrying from the kitchen.

"What is it, Miss Chandra?"

"It is Papa! I think he has had a heart-attack. We must send for the Doctor!"

"There's a boy at the back door with some groceries," Ellen replied, "I'll send him."

She hurried away and Chandra ran back to her father.

She knew there was very little she could do. She

undid his tie and loosened his collar, then felt his heart.

She was not experienced enough to know if it was irregular, but at least he was alive, and for the moment that was all that mattered.

*   *   *

It was two hours later when the Doctor came down the staircase with Chandra at his side.

"Your father is a lucky man," he said. "It was not a bad attack. Shall we say it is a warning, and he must be very much more careful in the future."

They reached the hall and he looked at the pile of luggage.

"I am afraid your father will be disappointed that he cannot go to Nepal," he said, "but a journey of any sort is out of the question."

Chandra did not speak, and he paused before he added:

"Unless, of course, he could spend the winter in a warm climate like the South of France."

He smiled and put his hand on Chandra's arm.

"I know, my dear, that is impossible, but I have just ordered that exact treatment for our Lord Lieutenant."

"Is Lord Dorrett ill?" Chandra enquired.

"He suffers from a combination of too rich living and not enough to do," the Doctor said with a smile, "although perhaps it is indiscreet of me to say so."

"That is something of which you could not accuse Papa," Chandra replied.

"No, and it is a pity that they cannot change places," the Doctor answered. "If your father could spend the winter in the warm sunshine and Lord Dorrett had as much work as the Professor manages to get through, they might both be healthier and longer-living men."

Chandra drew in her breath. Then she said:

"I have something to suggest to you."

It was after the Doctor had left that Chandra went upstairs to her father's bedroom, looking a little apprehensive.

He was lying against his pillows and she knew as she entered the room what he was going to say.

"If you have been listening to that old wind-bag," he said threateningly, "and intend to stop me from going to Nepal, you can save your breath!"

Chandra sat down on a chair by the bed.

"You are not going to Nepal, Papa," she said. "You are going to Cannes."

"To Cannes?" her father exclaimed. "What on earth are you talking about?"

"I have talked it over with Dr. Baldwin," Chandra said, "and he knows of a charming little Pension where you and Ellen will be happy and comfortable. He is also friendly with one of the local Doctors who will look after you."

"I think you have gone off your head!" her father retorted. "I am going to Nepal and no-one, you, Baldwin, or anyone else, is going to stop me!"

As Chandra did not speak, he went on:

"It is not only because I have been looking forward to the trip and because I wish to find the Lotus Manuscript. It is because, as you know, we need the money."

"We have the money."

"We can hardly keep it if I do not fulfil my obligations," her father replied.

"Now listen, Papa," Chandra said, bending forward to take his hand in hers. "I love you, and I do not intend to let you die on some Nepalese mountain when I am not with you. You know as well as I do that you could not undertake an arduous ride at this moment, with your heart in the condition it is."

"I have to, Chandra. I have to!"

"No," Chandra replied. "I have arranged everything, and I will not let you risk your life for the Lotus Manuscript. It is not worth it!"

She forced a smile to her lips as she said:

"It has existed for over two thousand years already, and whether you find it or not, it will doubtless go on existing for another two thousand!"

"What are you trying to say to me?" her father enquired.

Now his voice sounded suddenly weary, as if the spurt of energy he had put into defying her had left him exhausted.

"What I have decided," Chandra said quietly, "is that you shall go to the South of France with Ellen and I will go to Nepal in your place."

"Y-you?"

The word seemed to come jerkily from his lips.

"Why not?" Chandra asked. "You know as well as I do that I can recognise the age of a manuscript as competently as you can."

"Do you really imagine that Frome will take you with him?"

"He may refuse at the last moment," Chandra replied, "but by that time I shall have reached the borders of Nepal, and unless he is to go on alone, which I doubt, it will take him some time to find anybody as experienced as you ... or me, for that matter ... to accompany him."

Her father looked at her in astonishment, and then to Chandra's surprise he began to chuckle.

"I cannot believe that Frome will ever have found himself in such a difficult predicament," he said. "At the same time, it is something we cannot do."

"Why not?" Chandra asked.

"Because he has paid for my services."

"Whatever he has paid, he cannot have you because you are not fit enough to go with him," Chandra said, "and quite frankly, Papa, it is impossible for us to give him back his money, nor do I intend to do so."

The Professor shut his eyes for a moment and Chandra felt the hand she was holding go limp.

"It is—wrong!" he murmured.

"But it is something we have to do," Chandra said, "and I will not have you upsetting yourself about it. Just leave everything to me, Papa."

As she spoke, she felt that her father was deliberately slipping away in his thoughts from the problem that confronted him.

It was something he had often done in the past, when he had felt it was either too uncomfortable or too difficult to extricate himself from some awkward position or make a decision that was an unpleasant one.

Then it had been a mental evasion of facing the truth, but now she knew it was also a physical one.

His heart-attack had left him limp and very tired and he therefore did not wish to argue or even discuss difficulties to which he could find no solution.

"Leave everything to me, Papa," Chandra said again.

Then, feeling that he would sleep, she kissed him lightly on the forehead and drew down the blinds to shut out the afternoon sun.

Downstairs, as she had expected, she encountered far fiercer opposition from Ellen than anything she had heard from her father.

"If you're thinking you can go off alone on some wild-goose chase to one of those heathen, outlandish places that made your father ill in the first place, you can think again!" Ellen said firmly.

"You and Papa will have a lovely time in the South of France," Chandra replied. "Dr. Baldwin says he will be a different person by the time the winter is over."

"And what'll you be doing, I'd like to know?" Ellen asked angrily.

"I shall be earning the six hundred pounds which

Lord Frome gave to Papa and which we are not in a position to return."

"No decent young lady would go off alone, unchaperoned, and without even a maid with her."

"You can hardly expect me to take a lady's-maid riding over the mountains," Chandra answered, "and even if I agreed to take one, who would we find intrepid enough to accompany me?"

Ellen muttered something rude beneath her breath, and Chandra, who always knew how to handle the elderly woman, put her arm round her shoulders and said:

"Do not worry, Ellen. I can look after myself, and you know that Lord Frome is sending a servant to meet Papa at Bombay, so there will be somebody to see to the luggage."

"That's as may be!" Ellen admitted, who had seen the efficiency of a superior Indian servant. "But you're too young, and it's certainly not proper for you to be alone with a gentleman like Lord Frome."

"You need not worry about His Lordship," Chandra said with a smile. "Papa says he is a woman-hater, and I expect he will have a fit when he sees me anyway!"

"He looked a decent enough gentleman when I let him in the other afternoon," Ellen said grudgingly, "but one never knows."

"If he attacks me, which is extremely unlikely," Chandra said lightly, "I can always shoot him with Papa's pistol. I see you have included that in the baggage."

"Now, Miss Chandra, I'll not have you talking like that! It's not right or proper, and you know it's not. Send a cable to His Lordship, telling him your father's ill. After all, it's the only right thing to do."

"And if I do that," Chandra answered, "shall I put a post-script at the end, saying: *'Sorry we cannot return your money. Spent a great deal of it.'*?"

Ellen did not answer this question, and Chandra went on pressing her advantage:

"And what about Papa and the South of France? Dr. Baldwin said it is just what he needs, and you know as well as I do, Ellen, that the cough he had last winter would be the worst possible thing for his heart."

Ellen slapped down on the table the cloth that she had been holding in her hand.

"I don't know what the world's coming to, that I don't!" she said tartly, but Chandra knew she had won the argument.

It was, however, one thing to convince her father and Ellen that she had to go to Nepal, but something quite different to set off alone.

There was a feeling of exhilaration in it, and yet at the same time she was nervous.

It was not the travelling which alarmed her. She had travelled during her childhood and up to five years ago, when her mother had died, in all sorts of strange parts of the world.

She had been to India, and even though her father had been ill for some months and both she and her mother had found the heat of the Plains almost un-bearable, it was still a country that was always vividly in her thoughts.

It was exciting now to be going back to find if it was still as beautiful and as stimulating as it had been when she was very young.

What made her nervous was that when she arrived she might fail to persuade Lord Frome to let her take her father's place.

A further talk with Dr. Baldwin the following day had made her aware that for her father to regain his health, he required not only a change of atmosphere but far better food than he had been eating these past months.

Ellen was a good cook, but she could not cook what they could not afford to buy.

Although she had done wonders with eggs and vegetables, Dr. Baldwin insisted that the Professor's health
needed building up with foods which in general had
been too expensive for them to buy regularly.

Chandra found herself thinking of the second six
hundred pounds that Lord Frome had promised to pay
her father to work on the manuscript, if they found it.

There were so many things, so many comforts that
could be provided with such a sum in the bank, and
she was sensible enough to realise that the first six
hundred pounds would be spent by the end of the
winter.

"Lord Frome has to take me with him!" she told
herself.

She felt a little sinking feeling inside as she remembered the hard, authoritative note in his voice.

She was certain that he was the kind of man who
would think of no-one but himself and have no qualms,
if it suited him, about sending her home ignominiously.

The necessity was that it should not suit him.

He had to find her indispensable, just as he considered her father would be.

"I shall have to convince him," she told herself, but
she felt despairingly that she would be unable to do so.

* * *

Leaving home had been easier than she had anticipated, because her father had given up the unequal
struggle of arguing with her.

She knew it was because he felt far more ill than he
was prepared to admit and also had the honesty to admit that such an arduous journey at the moment was
completely impossible for him.

He would have remonstrated once more with Chandra, but she said to him quietly:

"There are only three things we can do, Papa. We
can wire Lord Frome that you are ill and unable to

join him, in which case we are under an obligation to return his money. Or I can go in your place, and if he refuses to take me with him into Nepal, then it will be his fault, and I will have no compunction about keeping every penny of the money he has given us already."

"And what is the third alternative?" her father asked.

Chandra laughed.

"There is not one, unless you have a brilliant idea!"

A faint smile came to the Professor's lips.

"For once you have set me a conundrum for which I have no answer," he said. "Perhaps your second idea is best."

"That is just what I have been saying," Chandra replied; "and if His Lordship is disagreeable, I can just say meekly that we tried to help him and it is not our fault that we failed."

However, she knew from her father's expression that he did not think Lord Frome would accept this argument.

As the ship set off from the dock at Southampton, she found herself feeling that every mile they travelled brought her nearer to a sinister and rather frightening man who was encroaching all the time upon her imagination.

Before she actually left the Manor there was too much to do that she had no time to think of anyone except her father and herself.

She and Ellen had been so busy preparing for his departure that it was an almost impossible task to change everything over for her.

Fortunately, at the same time as keeping all her father's equipment for travelling to the strange places they had visited for so many years, Ellen had also put away her mother's, and Chandra, having grown in the last five years, could now fit into them perfectly,

The riding-clothes and boots all might have been made for her, and were in fact made of far better material and had originally cost more than they could have afforded at the moment.

"The rest of your clothes are a disgrace, Miss Chandra," Ellen said disparagingly.

"I think it is unlikely that I shall need to wear anything that is attractive," Chandra answered, "and of course Mama's ordinary clothes are sadly out-of-date."

She smiled and added:

"Not that it would matter in Nepal."

She had, however, a feeling in the back of her mind that one thing Lord Frome would not want would be for her to look feminine or womanly.

She thought that perhaps the sensible walking-boots and ankle-length skirts that were suitable for mountaineering would be far more to his taste than the frilled gowns that she remembered the Mem-Sahibs wore in India in the evening, and the muslin dresses which graced them during the day.

Pressing things that had been folded away for such a long time until her back ached, Ellen grumbled and at the same time warned Chandra a thousand times a day of all the horrifying things that might happen to her.

It was not only the dangers of high mountains, wild animals, and bad food which concerned Ellen, but that there might be men who would be attracted to her and she would be defenceless and at their mercy without a chaperone to protect her.

"I have told you, Ellen, that I will keep them off with Papa's pistol," Chandra said.

"Now be sensible, Miss Chandra," Ellen replied. "Here's you, knowing nothing more about the world than a new-born baby, going off by yourself and meeting Heaven knows what sort of gentlemen in them outlandish places."

"I have told you, Ellen, there are no Europeans in Nepal since they are not allowed in. There will only be the British Resident, who is doubtless an old man with a white beard, and Lord Frome, who is a woman-hater."

She laughed and added:

"Instead of worrying what they will do to me, you ought to be hoping that I will meet Prince Charming riding over the mountains, who will sweep me off my feet and turn out to be a millionaire."

"I've always hoped that one day, Miss Chandra, you'd meet a nice young gentleman," Ellen said, "with a little bit of money, and settle down to a happy married life, which is something you are not likely to find in a country such as Nepal, wherever that might be."

Chandra laughed.

"You must get Papa to show you a map of it, Ellen; then you will be able to think of me surrounded by small dark men who will obviously think I look very queer to them, as they look to us."

"I don't know what your mother would say, that I don't!" Ellen exclaimed, as she had done a thousand times already, but Chandra knew that that was the end of that particular conversation.

When finally the moment came for her to drive away to the station, she felt curiously like crying.

It would have been so thrilling if she and her father could have gone together, but it was quite another thing to leave him behind and know that she would be alone during the long days at sea and the dusty, tiring journey from Bombay to the Nepalese border.

The one thing that did not trouble her father in the slightest was the idea of her travelling alone.

To him, it seemed as natural for her to ride up the side of the Himalayas as to walk to the village shops, and although Ellen fussed and fumed about her being unchaperoned, the idea that she might fall prey to lustful men never crossed her father's mind.

Chandra knew it was because in his estimation she was still the child she had always been, and an assistant in whose intelligence he was interested, but not her looks.

The night before she was to leave, she had sat in front of the mirror on the dressing-table and looked at herself critically.

She decided that if she behaved quietly and "kept herself to herself," as Ellen would have said, there would be no likelihood of her being worried by men approaching her because she was travelling alone.

She was aware that because she was doing so, the women would look at her questioningly and would doubtless not wish to make her acquaintance.

It was then that a sudden idea had come to her, and she had gone downstairs to say to Ellen:

"Would it make you happier about my journey to India if I went as a widow?"

"A widow, Miss Chandra? What do you mean by that?" Ellen asked.

"Well, you keep fussing because I have no chaperone, but if I were a widow I would not need one."

"But you're not a widow, so the question doesn't arise."

"What is to stop me from calling myself one and wearing Mama's wedding-ring? I saw it in her jewellery-box when we were unpacking her things."

"I've never heard such a ridiculous idea..." Ellen began, then she stopped. "There might be something in what you say, Miss Chandra."

"I think it is a sensible idea," Chandra said. "If anybody is so rude as to ask my age, I shall say I am twenty-three. At that age I can easily have been married and lost my husband in an accident. Or better still, on the Northwest Frontier. There is always fighting going on there."

She sat down at the kitchen-table with her chin in her hands.

"I know!" she exclaimed. "I shall call myself Mrs.

Wardell and pretend, while I am on board ship at any rate, that I was married to Papa's son."

"Your father never had a son!" Ellen corrected.

"We know that," Chandra agreed, "but the people on board ship will not have heard of Papa, so why should they know whether he had one or fifty children?"

It was an indisputable argument and finally Ellen agreed that a wedding-ring might be some form of protection, but she would not go so far, she added darkly, as to say what.

Accordingly, Chandra went aboard the steam-ship wearing her mother's wedding-ring and explained to the Purser that she had been forced to take her father-in-law's place because of his unexpected illness.

She was pleased to find that one of the best cabins had been engaged for her father on the First Class deck, and the stewards were very attentive in handling her luggage and arranging the cabin as she wished.

Chandra had travelled too often on small and un-comfortable ships in Second or Third Class accommo-dation not to appreciate the best when she found it.

She told herself that whatever else happened, even if she was sent home immediately she met Lord Frome, she would at least have the excitement of the journey to remember.

After the ship had left port, she went to the Dining-Saloon for dinner and looked at her fellow-passengers with interest.

It now took only seventeen days to reach India and she knew that for those seventeen days the people she was now looking at would be cooped together in a small world in which all the usual emotions and pas-sions of the great world outside would be enacted in miniature.

There would be sudden friendships and violent quar-rels, there would be those who would use shipboard acquaintances as a means of social promotion, and those who would isolate themselves for the very reason that they did not wish to be imposed upon.

There would also be those who would fall in love, and very likely out of love again, before the voyage ended.

"That," Chandra added to herself, "is something which is very unlikely to happen to me!"

Because she was travelling alone, she had been allotted a place at the First Officer's table. This was not as grand as the Captain's, which was kept for the most distinguished passengers.

There were several Army Officers and their wives returning to India after a short leave at home which they had doubtless spent with their children who had to be left behind, and two elderly ladies who were going out to stay with their sons and daughters who were married and settled in India.

There was one oldish man who looked as if he might be a scholar of some distinction, although Chandra was not sure, and two Officers who were apparently unattached, but she thought they did not appear to be the type whose intentions towards her would worry Ellen.

Immediately after dinner Chandra returned to her cabin.

As she unpacked the books she had brought with her, she told herself that the best thing she could do on the voyage was to concentrate on learning the language of Nepal, which her father had told her was different from those she had spoken in the past.

As was to be expected, the voyage was very much the same, if more comfortable, as those she had taken in the past.

There were bad storms in the Bay of Biscay, but the weather was warm and pleasant in the Mediterranean and extremely hot and humid in the Red Sea.

The food, which had seemed to be of high quality the first week at sea, gradually became monotonous and acquired a tastelessness which was characteristic of food that had been kept in cold-storage—a modern invention that had just been added to the P & O. Liners.

Although the other passengers did not ostracise Chandra in any respect, they did not go out of their way to solicit her friendship or make any kind of overtures that she found alarming or embarrassing.

She told herself that because they were a nondescript crowd she was nondescript too, and that was how she wanted it.

At the same time, when they reached the Red Sea and the stars were brilliant overhead she thought that nothing could be more romantic, except if she had someone to be romantic with.

It was only when they saw the outline of the Indian Continent that Chandra felt as if the overture to the play was over and now the curtain was rising on the drama itself.

At this point there was no need for her to go on with her pretence of being a widow, and she could be herself, her father's daughter, and persuade Lord Frome that she was as necessary to him as he believed her father to be.

The first step was to find Lord Frome's servant, and knowing how very important servants were to their Masters in India, Chandra knew it was something that she must tackle with charm and diplomacy.

Lord Frome's first report on her would come from the servant to whom he thought he was entrusting her father.

As the ship docked at Bombay there was the usual colourful crowd awaiting its arrival, the cheers and noise coming from the port, and little boats encircling the Steamer as if they were small fish escorting a whale.

Chandra moved from her cabin towards the Purser's office.

This, she knew, was where Lord Frome's servant would enquire for her father, and she waited, eyeing the crowds coming onto the ship and leaving it.

There was a kaleidoscope of colour, scarlet uniforms, yellow priestly robes, loin-cloths, saris, and turbans of every hue, and the noise of a thousand voices, like the Tower of Babel, shouting, it seemed, in a thousand different languages.

Then as Chandra waited, a man wearing a colourful turban approached the Purser's Office and she heard him ask for Professor Wardell.

She stepped forward.

"Have you come from Lord Frome?" she enquired.

He bowed and raised his hand to his forehead.

"I Mehan Lall, Mem-Sahib. The Lord Sahib send me meet Professor Wardell."

"I am the Professor's daughter," Chandra explained. "My father is ill and so I have come in his place. Will you please take me to Lord Frome?"

She saw the surprise on the Indian's face, and there was a distinct pause before he said:

"Mem-Sahib wish speak Lord Sahib? He not in Bombay."

"I know that," Chandra replied. "He was to meet my father at Bairagnia."

The Indian nodded.

"Then that is where I will see him."

"Mem-Sahib come to Bairagnia?"

"Yes," Chandra said firmly; "I am going to Nepal in my father's place."

Indian servants carry out instructions exactly as they are given, and they are not prepared to argue or to improvise. Chandra knew that if she was firm, the Indian would carry out his orders as efficiently as if he were attending her father.

She knew, however, that he was worried and perturbed that she was a lady and not, as he had expected, a gentleman.

He did not express his fears but merely collected her luggage, ordering the porters in a manner which made them hurry to do as he wished. When they left the Quay it was in a comfortable open carriage which had obviously been procured before the boat had docked.

As there was some time to wait before the train left, Mehan Lall took Chandra to a comfortable Hotel where she could rest and enjoy a cup of tea.

It was provided for her in the large, rather over-crowded Lounge, with all the ceremony that a meal required in England, and when she had finished Mehan Lall paid her bill and escorted her to the carriage which had been waiting with her luggage outside the Hotel.

They drove through the crowded streets of Bombay, which brought back memories of the India she had last known in the company of her father and mother.

But she could see that quite a lot of alterations had taken place in Bombay since she had last been there: there were many new buildings, new Hotels, improvements of the roads, but basically it was the same.

The Indians, in dhotis, saris, torn rags, nose-clips, ankle-bangles, turbans, topees, and bush-jackets, were all exactly as they had always been.

When she reached the railway-station she felt as if she had never been away.

There were the great trains with steam hissing up; the British engine-driver standing grandly at the cab of the mail-train locomotive; the British conductor with his check-board at the door of the First Class carriage; the British Stationmaster at the end of the platform, dressed in dark blue like an Admiral.

Of course there were British passengers like herself stalking down the platform in a miasma of privilege, with their servants and porters shouting and kicking out of the way the Indian passengers.

These were scrambling into the train for fear that it would leave without them, or eating or sleeping on piles of luggage which were not intended to leave the station until far into the dim future.

As Chandra expected, Lord Frome had engaged for her father a First Class carriage with a servants'-compartment next door.

Ellen had packed for her a padded quilt and a pillow, and Mehan Lall gave her a tiffin-basket, which Chandra was certain would contain whisky, soda-water, and perhaps some potted meats.

As usual in India, the comforts arranged for the conquerors of the country were superb and Chandra had nothing to do but step into the carriage and merely tell Mehan Lall where the porters were to put her various pieces of luggage which she would need on the journey.

When, with his usual polite bow and his hand touching his forehead, he left her, she sat down and pulled the blind over the window to shut out the hawkers shouting in hollow voices and peering at the travellers with beseeching eyes.

It was very hot. Chandra took off her hat and wiped her face, and as she did so, she felt the tension go out of her.

It had been somewhat of an ordeal, even though she had pretended to be very calm, to step onto Indian soil alone, to have her tea alone in the crowded Hotel, to travel alone to the station, and now to be alone in the train which would carry her from the western coast-line to the northeastern border, where Lord Frome would be waiting for her.

"If only Papa could be with me," she told herself again.

She knew they would have been laughing at the crowds on the station and enjoying every moment of being back in the India they had loved in the past.

But even without her father it was an adventure, and in case it did not last long Chandra told herself she was going to enjoy every moment of it.

The train started off with the wheels jerking and clattering and the wood-work creaking.

The noise from the platform with its hundreds of voices seemed to swell into a great crescendo of sound. Hands were waving, although whether to friends or to the train Chandra was not sure.

Then the train was accelerating its speed and carrying her away towards the land where the Himalayas stood with their snow-peaks vivid against the blue sky.

'Now I am really on my own,' she thought, and did not find it intimidating but instead stimulating, as if this was a new chapter in her life.

When she was aboard the ship everything had seemed to become familiar and repetitive.

Now when they stopped at railway-stations, large or small, Mehan Lall brought her food and drink. Her carriage was cleaned and made tidy for the day, and cleaned again and made comfortable for the night.

Mehan Lall telegraphed ahead for what she required to eat, and the moment they arrived at one of the stations, out of the shadows would appear a man dressed in white, carrying Chandra's luncheon or dinner on a tray covered with a napkin.

Whatever she ordered, the food always seemed to be the same, a fiery curry, chutney and onions, and *chupattis,* to be washed down with fresh lemonade, which was always either too acid or too sweet, never quite right.

Chandra remembered that she had to eat fast because before the train left the station the man in white required his plates back and of course to be paid.

As the train moved she could see him bowing perfunctorily as he retreated towards the food-stall.

On and on they journeyed, and now Chandra began to be thrilled by the ever-changing view.

They passed through plains and jungles, barren stony land, and green fields where water-bullocks pulled their ploughs and longed for the evening, when they could drop into the village pool and submerge themselves.

As they flashed past there were little scenes which remained in her memory almost like the views of a child's doll's-house.

A family of gypsies camped by the embankment, the metalsmiths of India, the women festooned in bangles, ear-rings, and anklets, their anvils beside them, their black tents pitched in the background.

Several children playing amongst a flock of small goats all so young that they seemed part of the enchantment of Pan or Krishna, the Indian god who also played his pipe of reeds.

There was always something new and exciting to see—a flickering oil-lamp on a village stall that hinted at unseen mysteries.

There would be long hours under the stars across plain-like land on which occasionally there would be the silhouette of a round-topped Mosque, or a caravan camped for the night beneath some overhanging rocks.

To Chandra it was all enchanting, all something that had been a part of her life in the past, and now she returned to it with the familiarity of a beloved parent.

On and on they journeyed, and now at last the air was much cooler and she required a blanket to cover her at night, while in the daytime she no longer felt stifled by the dry, airless heat.

On and on, until finally after an arid plain she saw in the distance the outline of the mountains.

Now she felt excited, but also apprehensive and afraid—much more afraid than she had before.

The train had changed engines when Chandra's carriage had been shunted onto the Bengal and North Western Railway and now was much smaller and the passengers were nearly all men, which was unusual in the lower part of India.

They were coming into Bairagnia and Chandra rose

to put on her sensible white hat and to look as she did so at her reflection in the mirror which was fitted into the carriage wall.

What would Lord Frome think when he saw her, she wondered, and knew without being told that his first reaction would be one of anger because not only was she not her father but she was also a woman.

Looking at her face, she wondered why he should dislike women so much.

She thought she looked quite inoffensive, in fact as she resembled her mother it was not conceited to know that she was attractive.

She had rather a serious look, perhaps because she had spent so much time studying.

Her small nose was straight and it lay between two large, very intelligent eyes: eyes that were grey in some lights and almost purple in others.

Her hair was not fair, and yet it was not dark. 'The colour of a pencil,' a girl had once said derogatorily.

Chandra thought that was a true description.

Her hair did look like a drawing that might have been made with a pencil and it was unfashionably straight instead of curly, as most girls took endless trouble to ensure with crimping tongs.

There was just a gentle wave in Chandra's hair, which parted in the middle and fell on either side of an oval, intelligent-looking forehead.

Although she did not realise it, it was a face that would make a man who was interested in her look and look again; a face that would be difficult to forget; a face that could haunt someone who stared at it for too long.

But because she did not parade herself as other women did, because in many ways she did not make the best of her looks, Chandra, like an exquisite drawing, could be overlooked when there were colourful and larger pictures round.

Only those who sought quality would really appreciate the lines of her face, which bespoke good bones, and see that her eyes had a depth that was not to be found in most women.

Chandra saw little of this. All she was concerned with was what would be Lord Frome's first impression, and that, she told herself, was something she would find out in the next few minutes.

She pushed her hair under her hat, and though she was very simply dressed, she wished she were wearing riding-clothes because they would look more service-able and perhaps more masculine.

Then her sense of humour made her laugh.

If she attempted to look like a man for Lord Frome, she was bound to fail. He had to accept her or repudiate her as she was. It was not her appearance which should concern him but her intelligence.

Slowly, letting off an immense amount of steam, the train came into the station.

It was a small station and therefore there were not the huge crowds there had been in Bombay or at other stations where they had stopped en route.

But there were the usual Indian sightseers, the usual family that would be travelling not today, not tomorrow, but perhaps in a week's time, who had settled down to live in the station in the meantime just in case they missed the "puffing monster dragon," of which they were so frightened.

Chandra saw Mehan Lall come to the door of her carriage.

He opened it preparatory to speaking to her, and as he did so she heard the voice she had heard before in her father's Study say:

"Here you are, Mehan Lall, and only three hours late, which must be a record! Where is the Professor?"

As he spoke, Lord Frome stepped in through the open door of the carriage.

He saw Chandra and froze in his tracks.

"I beg your pardon," he murmured. "There has been a mistake."

"There is no mistake, Lord Frome," Chandra replied, holding out her hand. "My name is Wardell. I am Professor Wardell's daughter."

"Professor Wardell's daughter?"

Lord Frome spoke slowly, as if he was keeping control of his voice, and as he spoke he looked round the carriage.

"And where is your father?"

"That is something I have to explain to you," Chandra replied. "Do you wish to hear it now, or when we have left the train?"

She thought for one moment that Lord Frome would rebuke her for her impertinence. Then he asked, and his voice was sharp and abrupt:

"Are you telling me that your father did not come with you?"

"He is in England."

Lord Frome's lips tightened and for the first time Chandra was able to look directly at him, taking in his appearance.

He was good-looking, she thought, decidedly so, in a hard, impersonal manner which made her think that she had been right in disliking him even when she had only heard his voice.

He was tall, broad-shouldered, and in a way very English, and yet there was something else, something which seemed to exude from him almost like waves of magnetism.

It was an authority, a determination, or a will-power, Chandra was not certain which, or perhaps all three, but it made him awe-inspiring even though she told herself that there was no reason why he should be.

"Very well, Miss Wardell," he said sharply. "Of course I wish to hear your explanation, and perhaps it would be best for me to take you to the Dak-Bunga-low where I am staying."

Chandra thought for a moment that, as if taken by surprise, his voice was not so peremptory as it had been previously.

She had the feeling that if it was possible, he would have liked her to stay on the train. But as this was obviously impossible, he had to invite her to the Bungalow, which she suspected would be somewhat inadequate.

Without waiting for him to say any more, Chandra stepped out of the train, noting as she did so that while Mehan Lall stood with the luggage already heaped on the backs of two porters, he was watching his Master apprehensively.

"Shall I lead the way?" Lord Frome asked, and without waiting for Chandra's reply he stepped into the crowd.

They seemed to move aside for him almost as if he deliberately swept them from his path, and as Chandra followed him she thought with a smile that she was like the Eastern women who had eternally to walk humbly two paces behind their men.

'He is angry with me,' she thought, 'and yet for the moment there is nothing he can do about it.'

Lord Frome reached the front of the station. Chandra saw the usual collection of beggars holding out their hands optimistically, but really without much hope that anyone would pay any attention to them.

Then ahead only a very short distance from the station she saw what was obviously a Dak-Bungalow or Rest House.

It was in fact larger than she had expected, and she knew exactly what the rooms would be like inside, for the Dak-Bungalows which had been erected all over India by the British were invariably designed on the same pattern.

It suddenly struck her that in such a small place as

Bairagnia the Bungalow might contain only one bedroom and one Sitting-Room, in which case Lord Frome
might find it difficult to accommodate her even for
the night.

Then as they walked across the soft, sandy ground,
Chandra saw that her fears were groundless. The Bungalow was big enough to provide rooms for three or
perhaps four visitors.

As far as she was concerned she wanted only one
room to herself.

Lord Frome, who was still walking a pace or so
ahead, stepped onto the verandah.

There were several chairs with a small iron table
between them but he opened the door and went into
the building.

Here there was the inevitable wooden-walled room
with a square table and several hard chairs.

Most people, unless they were eating, sat outside on
the verandah.

Lord Frome drew out a chair from the table and
sat down at it. Then, looking at Chandra as she stood
just inside the door, he said in his hard, authoritative
voice:

"And now, Miss Wardell, perhaps you will tell me
exactly why you are here."

Chapter Three

Chandra sat down opposite Lord Frome, realising as she did so that he had not invited her to sit, and she wondered if he intended her to stand in front of him like a servant.

In a voice which she forced to sound quiet and slow, she said:

"Unfortunately, my father had a heart-attack two days before he was due to leave."

"You did not cable me!"

"No," Chandra responded. "And because I thought that it would be very difficult for you to find anyone quickly to replace my father, I came in his place."

For a moment Lord Frome looked at her incredulously. Then he said:

"By what possible reasoning could you believe that you could be of any use to me?"

Chandra smiled.

She had thought that this would be his attitude, and she replied:

"For the last five years I have worked with my father on the Sanskrit manuscripts. I can say without conceit that my ability to translate is nearly as good as his, and therefore considerably better than that of anyone else you would be able to employ at a moment's notice."

"That would be for me to decide," Lord Frome snapped.

"My father and I were in fact thinking for you," Chandra said. "We knew how hard it would be, once you reached here, to find someone to ride with you to Nepal."

"And you are prepared to do that?"

"I have travelled a great deal with my father in the past," Chandra replied, "and I do not expect that Nepal will be much different from any other country."

"You must be quite mad," Lord Frome said rudely, "if you really think I can arrive in Nepal accompanied by a woman."

"Perhaps you could think of me not as a woman but as a substitute for my father, and someone who would be able to identify the Lotus Manuscript as well as he could."

"That I can hardly believe," Lord Frome replied. "In fact, to tell you the truth, Miss Wardell, you have stretched my credulity too far for me to believe anything you say."

"Perhaps you would like to put me to a test," Chandra suggested. "Give me a Sanskrit manuscript and I will translate it for you."

Lord Frome suddenly brought down his fist hard on the table in front of him as he said:

"This whole situation is absurd, utterly absurd. I wished your father to come with me to Nepal to identify the Lotus Manuscript because he is the greatest Sanskrit scholar in the world. You can hardly expect me to accept as a substitute a young girl with no experience, even if she is his daughter."

"I am older than I look," Chandra said, remembering that on the voyage she was to pass herself off as twenty-three.

"That is not the point!" Lord Frome retorted, as if he resented her having an answer to everything he said.

"The point, surely, is that I can do what you want," Chandra insisted. "Whether you believe it or not, I am very experienced in the translation of Sanskrit. I can also recognise as accurately as my father the age of a manuscript, and that is the particular reason why you wanted him to accompany you to Nepal."

This was irrefutable, and Lord Frome, glowering at her as if he suspected that she had an ulterior motive for everything she said, suddenly rose to his feet and walked restlessly across the small room to the window.

He stood looking out at the bright crimson of a bougainvillaea but Chandra was certain that in actual fact he did not see it.

He was merely contemplating the collapse of his plans and being extremely angry that things were not going as smoothly as he had hoped.

She remembered all too well how confident he had sounded when talking to her father, when he had said he had planned everything ahead and if things went wrong he wished to know the reason why.

In this case the reason was quite simple. Her father was too ill to join him and so she had come in his place.

She almost wanted to say it out loud to him, as if reading an easy primer to a child, but she thought that that would make him only more angry.

Therefore she just sat still, her hands in her lap, hoping that she looked studious and not in the least a frivolous type of woman who might disturb him.

There was a long silence while Lord Frome stood with his back to her. Then he said, as if he had not come to any positive decision:

"Even if I agree to you accompanying me in your father's place, it would be impossible, as I have already said, for me to arrive in Katmandu accompanied by a young woman who was unchaperoned."

Chandra thought, with a little smile of amusement, that it might have been Ellen speaking.

"I should not have thought that a chaperone was necessary in such an obscure part of the world," she remarked.

She knew, even as she spoke, that nothing was too far away or obscure for gossip, and as Lord Frome was a man of distinction what happened in Katmandu would doubtless sooner or later be gossiped about over the tea-cups in Simla.

"I still think it is extremely reprehensible of you not to have sent me a cable," Lord Frome said suddenly, as if his mind was off on another tack.

"One very good reason why I did not do so," Chandra replied, "was because you did not give my father an address. I daresay it would have found you here, but if you had then suggested that I should come in his place, there would have been a long delay before I could reach you."

"I should have suggested nothing of the sort!" Lord Frome retorted. "There are other Sanskrit scholars who would doubtless have been only too pleased to take this trip with me."

Chandra made no reply but merely sat quietly. After a time Lord Frome turned towards her, and she could see by the expression on his face how angry he was.

"I shall have to think this over, Miss Wardell," he said. "It is not a decision I can make in a few seconds."

He paused to look at her aggressively, as if he expected her to argue, then he continued:

"You will obviously have to stay the night here, and as there will be no train back until mid-day tomorrow, I can give you my decision as to whether or not you can stay at breakfast tomorrow, which I have ordered at six o'clock."

"Thank you," Chandra said.

As she spoke she rose to her feet, and as she did so she felt that Lord Frome was watching her almost as if he thought he might discover by his scrutiny something he did not know already.

He made her feel self-conscious but at the same time she hoped that she did not show it.

She merely walked to the door, and as she did so Lord Frome said:

"I presume you will want to eat. My man-servant is preparing a meal at this moment."

"Thank you," Chandra said again, and walked from the room out to the verandah.

There was another door, which she thought must lead to the bedrooms, and she found that she was not mistaken.

There were three very small rooms side-by-side and she found that Mehan Lall had already put her things in the first of them.

The Dak-Bungalows were always primitive but clean, and in each bedroom was a *charpoy,* or native bed, which consisted of a frame with cross-webbing on four legs, on which travellers placed their own bedding.

A plain chest-of-drawers, a chair, and a table on which there was a candle, for when it grew dark, constituted the rest of the furnishings.

At the back of the building there was a washing-sluice, which the keeper kept supplied with a number of cans of cold water.

When she had undressed, a little shyly because she was afraid that she might meet Lord Frome, Chandra went to the sluice and washed.

She felt cleaner and cooler after she had done so. Then she went back to her room and put on a plain gown that she hoped made her look severe and business-like.

With its little white collar it was almost **Puritanical**
in appearance. She dragged her hair into a small, tight
bun at the back of her head and even tried to smooth
away the two waves that fell on either side of her forehead.

"If I had been sensible," she told her reflection in
the mirror, "I would have brought with me a pair of
spectacles, even though I do not need them."

She knew that a great deal would depend on what
Lord Frome thought of her when they ate together.

At the moment she was very uncertain as to whether
he would submit to what she hoped he would find inevitable and take her with him to Nepal.

She knew that his instinct was to send her back immediately on the train tomorrow. At the same time,
she was hoping that he would find it so inconvenient
to have no expert in Sanskrit with him that he would
accept her because there was no ready alternative.

She was certain, however, that he was the type of
man whose reactions one could never anticipate, and,
as she had thought when she had first heard his voice,
there was something hard and ruthless about him.

She was sure that he was completely selfish when it
came to his own interests.

She had hurried over washing and changing simply
because she felt that to keep him waiting might make
her appear to be typically feminine.

She felt a sense of relief when she went back into
the Sitting-Room and found that he was not there.

A servant was laying the table and there was a clean
white cloth over it which inevitably was rough-dried.
In the centre of the table a wicker-basket was filled
with *chupattis* and other types of Indian bread.

The servant bowed to her when she appeared. Then,
before Chandra could speak as she intended to do,
Lord Frome came into the room.

She saw at once that he had changed, as she had,
and in a way, because he was conventionally clad for

the evening, it made him seem more awe-inspiring and even more authoritative than he had been in his riding-clothes.

"What will you drink, Miss Wardell?" he asked abruptly. "I am afraid that as I was expecting your father, your choice is limited to whisky or Indian beer."

"I like Indian beer," Chandra replied, "and it will be delightful to drink it again."

"You have been in India before?"

"I was with my father in various parts of the country six years ago."

She thought Lord Frome looked at her speculatively, as if he thought she was lying because she would have been too young at the time. But he did not say anything, except to order the servant to bring her a glass of beer while he himself ordered a whisky.

They sipped their drinks in silence until the food was ready, and then sat down at the table.

What they ate was, Chandra thought, the inevitable travellers' menu: hot soup; a very skinny chicken which, having been killed only a few hours earlier, was very tough, and yet cooked with spices it was quite appetising; and a caramel pudding.

This was one of the dishes that all English Mem-Sahibs taught their Indian servants and it appeared monotonously at every meal for Europeans.

Because she thought it was polite, Chandra said after they had sat in silence for some time:

"Your servant is a good cook."

"He does his best," Lord Frome replied, "and when I am travelling I am not really interested in what I am eating."

Chandra thought that this was true.

There was a preoccupied expression on his face which told her that he was thinking of other things while he consumed what was put in front of him.

She wondered if she should tell him that she was a very good cook and suggest that in an emergency she could, if he liked, provide something very different from what they had just eaten.

Then she thought that that was the last thing she should say: it would sound far too feminine and far too obviously like she was trying to encroach upon his bachelor mode of existence.

Instead she sat silently, and only as they finished did Lord Frome say:

"I want to talk to you, Miss Wardell. I suggest we go out onto the verandah."

"That will be very nice," Chandra replied, and walked outside.

The sun had sunk but there was the golden translucent glow in the sky that comes before darkness.

As she sat down on one of the wicker chairs she could hear the crickets chirping in the surrounding shrubs.

She listened to them as she looked out over the dusty road which led down to the station and to where in the distance there was a little cultivated land and beyond that sand and barren rocks.

It was all so familiar and so dear that Chandra felt as if she had come home.

Behind the Bungalow there was the distant chatter of voices, a baby crying, and the creak of a well-wheel.

There was the smell of warm dust and stones that had been sun-soaked all day and the scent of woodsmoke. Then as Chandra felt her whole being moving like a wave of love towards it all, Lord Frome came and sat down beside her.

"I have been thinking over your extraordinary, if I may say so, behaviour in coming here without informing me what you intended to do," he said slowly. "As I am quite certain you are aware, Miss Wardell, you have put me in an extremely difficult position."

There was no doubt of the hostility in his voice and it seemed to Chandra to grate harshly on what she had been feeling.

With an effort she turned her eyes towards him, thinking it was polite to appear as if she was listening, while she longed to return to her contemplation of the view and to listen to the sounds that were so peculiarly Indian.

"My first impulse," Lord Frome went on, "is to send you home immediately with a letter to your father saying that he should never have allowed you to come in the first place. Unfortunately, I have other factors to consider."

He paused and Chandra could see what she thought was almost an expression of hatred in his eyes, then he said:

"I have permission to enter Nepal for a short time, and my permit, if that is the right word, begins in three days, when I intend to reach Katmandu."

His lips tightened, and there was no need for him to explain that it had taken months of negotiation to obtain permission to enter the country. If he had to start all over again, he might be delayed for a further two or three months—or perhaps longer.

Chandra felt a little thrill of hope raise its head excitedly inside her.

She had forgotten, while pressing on Lord Frome the advantage of taking her in her father's place, that the question of a permit to enter a closed country was a very important one.

"I could, of course, cancel my whole journey indefinitely," Lord Frome was saying, "but I very much dislike having to change my plans, and I have in fact been determined for a long time to spend these next few months in Nepal."

"I can assure you," Chandra said in a voice that was as cold as his, "that my father was deeply disappointed at not being able to accompany you, and even the fact that the journey might have killed him would not have deterred him, if it had been physically possible for him to come with you."

"I had no idea that the Professor was in ill-health," Lord Frome said almost resentfully.

"My father is not as young as he was when he made his expeditions to Tibet and Sikkim," Chandra said, "and I think you may find later, My Lord, that on expeditions of this sort, one ages quickly."

If she had meant to startle Lord Frome, she had succeeded.

"Do you think that is true?" he enquired.

"I know it is," Chandra replied. "My father has had malaria a number of time, and of course various types of Asiatic fever, which take their toll of even the strongest men and certainly sooner or later affect the heart."

She knew that this was something else which Lord Frome had not considered, but as she spoke she thought that he looked very young, and people with robust health seldom thought of the frailty of others.

"Your father has been so helpful to me in the past," Lord Frome said a little grudgingly, "and I am afraid I never considered his age."

"I think that perhaps," Chandra said, "you do not consider him as a person at all, but merely as someone who was very useful to you."

If she had meant to shock him, Lord Frome could not have looked more surprised.

"I consider that a most unfair assertion," he protested.

She did not argue but merely bowed her head a little, as if to acknowledge his retort, but she did not reply to it.

"Let us return to what we were discussing," Lord Frome said sharply, "which is whether or not you shall accompany me to Nepal. I wish I could be convinced, Miss Wardell, that you are as competent in your work as you tell me you are."

"My father is extremely satisfied with what I do for him," Chandra replied. "In fact, the last manuscript you sent him, the *Bhadravadana,* I translated entirely myself; my father merely revised it."

She thought, from the way Lord Frome looked at her, that he very much doubted that this was true, but aloud he said:

"There is nothing I can do but take your word for your capabilities, in which case the problem is how I can justify your travelling with me, seeing that you are not only a woman but young in years."

"Time, of course, will eradicate one of those difficulties," Chandra said; "the second is, unfortunately, unchangeable."

She had spoken without thinking, and she knew that Lord Frome was surprised. She was afraid that he might think she was being flippant.

She was beginning to find his pomposity and the manner in which he openly revealed his dislike of her so irritating that she longed to say that she had no intention of going with him to Nepal or anywhere else in the world.

But all the time at the back of her mind she was remembering how much they needed the money.

It would be difficult to return even part of the six hundred pounds, which by now had paid for her father and Ellen's tickets to Cannes, and provided them for some weeks with their board and lodgings in the Pension which Dr. Baldwin had chosen for them.

Because she disliked having to toady to Lord Frome, with an effort she managed to say in a humble tone:

"If Your Lordship will be kind enough to take me with you to Katmandu, I promise you I will do everything in my power to see that I am as unobtrusive as possible."

"You will still be there with me," Lord Frome said grimly, "and we have to think of how it will appear to the outside world."

Chandra longed to argue that the "outside world"

was so far away that it really was rather foolish to worry about it.

Then she remembered that as Lord Frome was so important, he obviously had to be concerned with his reputation, while hers was of no consequence.

It seemed to her, however, that he was making a great fuss about nothing.

Famous men from the beginning of time had travelled with their mistresses, and in India all the Maharajahs had a number of concubines who accompanied them wherever they went.

But obviously Lord Frome, who was a woman-hater, was making certain that he not only had no contact with women but was never talked about in relation to them.

After a moment Chandra said a little hesitatingly:

"I . . . I suppose it would not be . . . possible for me to disguise myself as . . . a boy or a young . . . man?"

"Good God, no!" Lord Frome exclaimed. "That sort of play-acting would not deceive anybody! No, Miss Wardell, I am afraid what we have to do is more drastic, for I can find no other possible means by which I can justify taking you with me to Katmandu."

Chandra looked at him in surprise and he said:

"I assure you it is not anything I would even consider at any other time or place, but this is an exceptional problem, simply because I cannot afford to wait and find somebody else to take your father's place."

"What . . . are you suggesting?" Chandra enquired.

"It is quite simple," Lord Frome replied, in a voice which made it quite clear that it was nothing of the sort. "It is that you should come with me to Katmandu as my wife!"

Now it was Chandra's turn to look astonished, and her eyes widened as she stared at him.

"Of course it will be a pretence only for the time we are there," Lord Frome said quickly, as if he was afraid that she thought he might be proposing to her, "but it will obviate any questions that the British Resident, Colonel Wylie, might ask, and it will be an excuse for your presence which no-one will question."

"Your . . . wife?" Chandra said in a low voice.

This was something she had never anticipated in her wildest dreams.

"I can assure you, Miss Wardell," Lord Frome said in a bitter voice, "it is the type of deception that I would greatly deplore in any other circumstances, but this is undoubtedly an emergency which has never occurred before in my life, and which I fervently hope will never happen again."

"B-but . . . surely . . . ?" Chandra began.

Then, as she thought of it, she realised that it was, from Lord Frome's point of view, a very sensible idea.

She could imagine, because of his hatred of women, how he would loathe the innuendoes, the snide remarks, and the assumptions even by his servants that because there was a woman with him, she was his mistress.

To put a respectable front on it, to appear as man and wife, was to take any immoral aspect or indeed any romance out of the situation and make it just an ordinary journey in which a wife automatically accompanied her husband wherever his duties or interests took him.

That was not the spirit in which her father and mother had travelled, but she knew that they had been exceptional.

The majority of wives in India, or anywhere else in the East, followed where their husbands' occupations carried them, grumbling and complaining but nevertheless having little or no say in where they must set up another temporary home.

"I do not need to assure you," Lord Frome was saying, "that if the idea is abhorrent to you, it is even more so to me, and perhaps I should add that I am an avowed bachelor."

Chandra thought he was making it very clear that she should not "cast her cap" at him, and she longed to reassure him that he was quite safe in that respect.

'A more disagreeable, unpleasant man I have yet to meet!' she thought. 'I can only hope that my husband, when I have one, is not in the least like Lord Frome.'

Aloud she said, in a reluctant tone:

"I suppose Your Lordship is right in thinking that it is the only . . . possible way I can accompany you. At the same time, I admit it is not a situation that I look forward to with any pleasure."

"Pleasure!" Lord Frome ejaculated. "You cannot think it gives me any pleasure?"

He stared at her for a moment, then said in a quieter tone:

"It is just a measure of expediency, and I hope you will treat it as such."

"You need have no fears on that account," Chandra said coldly, "and as it happens, I thought that as I had no chaperone, I would be wise on the ship to say I was a widow. I therefore travelled as Mrs. Wardell."

As if he was forced against his will to find it amusing, just for a moment there was a slight twinkle in Lord Frome's eyes as he said:

"So you have already found the marriage status a convenient disguise?"

"Before I left England I thought it might be," Chandra answered, "but actually I need not have troubled. There was nobody on the ship who paid me any attention that I could possibly resent."

"I can assure you that the situation will be the same in Nepal," Lord Frome said.

"Thank you."

As Chandra spoke, she rose to her feet.

"If Your Lordship will excuse me, I would like to retire early. I presume, as you have made the decision as to what we shall do, we shall leave immediately after breakfast."

"We have a long ride in front of us, Miss Wardell," Lord Frome replied, as he too rose from the chair on which he had been sitting.

"I will be ready," Chandra replied.

She passed him on the verandah, then turned back to say:

"Perhaps I should thank you for taking me with you and express my hope that you will not regret it."

"I wish I could be sure of that," Lord Frome replied.

For a moment she thought there was a faintly mocking smile on his lips.

She bowed her head as she said:

"Good-night, My Lord."

"Good-night, Miss—Wardell!"

There was just the slightest pause before he said her surname, and she knew he was thinking that he would have to address her differently on the morrow.

As she walked through the door which led to her bedroom, Chandra knew with amusement that Lord Frome was wondering what was her Christian name.

"I will not tell him," she decided; "I will make him ask me!"

* * *

Chandra's bedroom seemed hot despite the fact that outside it was very much cooler.

She opened the windows and stood looking out, thinking how friendly and familiar it all was, until Lord Frome interrupted her on the verandah.

She saw a woman walking up the road, with a basket on her head. She was not young, but she walked with the carriage and grace of a Queen.

'Tomorrow,' Chandra thought, 'I shall enter a new land! It will all be an exciting adventure because it is strange and unusual, and a place I have never been before.'

She knew, in that moment, how afraid she had been that Lord Frome would send her home and she would never see Nepal or the Lotus Manuscript.

It was not only a question of the money which she wanted for her father's sake, but also for her own.

Because the tension was over now, she felt that she must go down on her knees and say a prayer of thankfulness because she had won the battle which she might so easily have lost.

"Thank you . . . thank you," she said in her heart, instinctively raising her face to the sky as she did so.

Then she heard a whisper:

"Mem-Sahib! Mem-Sahib!"

As she looked down, she felt as if she came back to earth with a thump as she saw a small Indian boy standing outside the window.

He had the huge, dark, liquidy eyes and appealing expressions of Indian children which she had seen thousands of times, and yet this had never failed to pull at her heart-strings.

They were so beautiful, and yet with their small bones and soft brown bodies, they were so vulnerable and fragile.

"Mem-Sahib! Come! Holy Man speak you!"

The boy spoke almost incomprehensible English, and Chandra replied in Urdu:

"What are you saying? Who is it who wants me?"

The small boy was obviously delighted that she could speak his own language.

"Holy Man, very great Holy Man, want speak with Mem-Sahib. Come now!"

"But how? And where is he?" Chandra asked, bewildered.

The small boy pointed, but from the window she could not see at what his finger was directed.

"Come, Mem-Sahib! Very important!" the boy said again.

Because Chandra was intrigued she replied:

"Wait for me. I will join you as soon as I can."

She shut the window, went to the door of her bed-room, and listened before she opened it.

There was no sound outside, and she knew that the doors of the other two bedrooms were closed.

She slipped past them and the sluice and went out through the back door of the Bungalow.

She was certain that if Lord Frome had not gone to bed, he would still be on the verandah where she had left him.

At the back of the Bungalow was the well, a few untidy shrubs, and beyond that some insignificant buildings which she knew housed the caretaker and his family.

She turned the corner and found the small boy waiting for her.

He smiled at her, obviously delighted that she had come, then set off through the shrubs and bushes to where on the edge of the garden surrounding the Bun-galow there were several trees.

As she followed him, Chandra found herself won-dering what all this could be about; at the same time, she thought that perhaps she was being rather rash in leaving without telling anybody where she was going.

However, she had no desire to confide in Lord Frome, and she told herself that there could be no possible danger in this quiet place inhabited only by people who served the railway-station.

She moved on a very short way before she saw that the small boy, who had scampered ahead, was stand-ing in front of a man who was seated under a large tree.

As Chandra drew nearer, she saw that it was a Holy Man who was waiting for her, and she recog-nised at once that he was from the hills.

When they had been in India, men whom her father had known in Tibet had come to see him even as far south as Bombay.

Chandra had learnt to know many of the hundreds of different Indians, but there were none more outstanding than the Holy Men from the North.

The man sitting at the foot of the tree was tall and was dressed in a robe, shaped like a coat, which was made of thick wool like a blanket.

His turned-back hat, not unlike a Mandarin's, was edged with fur, at his belt hung a wooden rosary, and there was an expression on his face that was unmistakable.

It was difficult to describe, and yet to Chandra it immediately made him a man of dedication, one of those who spent their whole lives intoning the sacred words in the great Lamaseries that her father had visited in Tibet.

The Holy Man made no effort to rise or even speak as she approached him, and because she knew that it was expected of her, she put her hands together.

Palm to palm, finger to finger, she raised them to her forehead in the traditional greeting of *Namaskar,* which the Indians gave to Gurus or to others whom they considered Holy.

"Greetings, daughter!" the Holy Man said, in a voice far deeper than any Southern Indian could have attained. "It is with distress that I learn that your Honourable father is ill."

"How do you know that?" Chandra asked in surprise, and even as she spoke she knew that it was a ridiculous question.

Of course, it would already be known in Bairagnia that her father had been expected and she had come in his stead.

"I have had the acquaintance of your Honorable father."

Chandra's eyes lit up.

"You know my father?" she exclaimed. "How interesting! What is your name?"

"I am the Lama Teshoo from the Sakya-Cho Monastery," the Holy Man replied.

"I am sure I remember my father speaking of your Monastery. It is in Tibet?"

The Lama nodded.

"Yes, Tibet, where your Honorable father visited us ten years ago."

"Then you must be disappointed that he is not here now," Chandra said. "He had a heart-attack at the last moment and could not come."

"He is in capable hands," the Lama said slowly, "and will live for many more years before he is released."

He spoke so positively that Chandra believed him and smiled.

"But as your father is not here," the Lama said, "I must ask you, his daughter, for your help."

"My help?" Chandra enquired.

The Lama nodded.

Chandra wondered how old he was. She had the feeling that, like so many Holy Men whose faces and bodies do not age as do those of ordinary people, he was very old in years.

"Tomorrow," he said, "you will be leaving with the Lord Sahib for Nepal."

Chandra thought it extraordinary that he should be so certain of this when she herself had not known of it until a few minutes ago.

But she made no comment and the Lama went on:

"When you are in Katmandu there is something you can do for our Monastery which will bring great merit to you in this life and in those which follow."

"What is it that you want me to do?" Chandra asked.

The old Lama gestured to her to come nearer and

sit at his feet, and she knew that what he had to say was secret.

The small Indian boy, without having been told to do so, had moved out of ear-shot and was lying on some tufts of grass, playing with a piece of wood.

The Lama seemed to think for some minutes before he said:

"You know who I mean when I speak of Nana Sahib?"

Chandra thought for a moment, then said:

"Do you mean the Rajah of Bithur who behaved with such incredible cruelty during the Indian Mutiny?"

The Lama nodded, and though she could not imagine how Nana Sahib could concern her in Nepal, Chandra remembered that he had in fact been the perpetrator of one of the most cruel and treacherous acts of the whole Indian Mutiny.

The beleaguered British Garrison at Cawnpore had been offered by Nana Sahib a safe passage to Allahabad if they were prepared to lay down their arms.

The English Officers in charge of the Fort would themselves have wished to hold on until a relief-force arrived.

However, they had no choice. Rations and ammunition were almost exhausted and the women and children were in a desperate state.

Finally, though they had mental reservations, they trusted Nana Sahib, who in the past had always appeared to be very sympathetic towards the English.

Forty large boats were provided at a landing-place, and at dawn the survivors of the siege, with their clothes in rags and stained with blood and dust, were taken to the boats in a procession of sixteen elephants followed by seventy to eighty palanquins and bullock-carts for the wounded.

It was in the minds of all the Officers that it might be a trick, but they proceeded to the boats, which were moored where the Ganges ran between high brown banks.

When they reached the river, they found that nothing had been provided to help the women and children to embark and there were no means of carrying aboard the sick and wounded.

The men and women waded into the deep and muddy water while the native boatmen and bearers watched in ominous silence.

By eight o'clock in the morning the boats were crowded with human beings panting in the white heat of the morning and taunted constantly by the mutineers from the shore.

They were almost ready to leave when, promptly at nine o'clock, as if at a signal, the boatmen deserted their boats and leapt overboard.

Instantly, firing started from both sides of the river, a withering fusillade of musket and cannon, setting on fire the thatched roofs of the boats.

The women screamed and struggled to protect their children from the shots which churned the river to foam, while the sweating, frantic men tried to push the boats forward but were cut down and fell into the blood-flecked water.

Lighted braids were thrust against the clothing of the women, and the children were smashed to the ground, their brains dashed by iron-tipped clubs.

Of those left behind in Cawnpore, all the men were killed and 206 women and children were imprisoned under ghastly conditions.

Finally when Nana Sahib's armies were defeated by the releasing forces, five out of the nine hundred men, women, and children, only five were alive.

The severed heads, limbs, and mutilated bodies had been thrown into a well close-by.

"I have faced death in every form," one man wrote, "but I could never look down that well again."

It was this treachery which had turned the British

Army, when they heard of it, into avengers inspired by a fiery crusade.

"Yes, of course, I remember hearing of Nana Sahib," Chandra said.

"When the relief forces reached Cawnpore," the Lama went on, "many thousands had to flee to save their lives, and the nearest place of refuge was Nepal."

Chandra looked up intently.

She was beginning to see where the conversation was leading.

"Among the refugees was Nana Sahib."

"He hid in Nepal?" Chandra exclaimed. "But I thought Nepal had favoured England during the mutiny and had offered soldiers to fight for the British."

"That is true," the Lama said, "and at the same time, the Prime Minister, Jang Bahadur, had a warm friendship for Britain. All the same, he allowed Nana Sahib to shelter unofficially in his country."

"But he must now have been dead for a long time," Chandra said.

"There were many reports of his death," the Lama said quietly, "but they were untrue."

Chandra looked surprised, and he went on:

"His wife, or the woman believed to be the widow of Nana Sahib, lived on the outskirts of Katmandu for over forty years. She was beautiful but also pious, and every year on a specific date she fed many religious mendicants."

Chandra wondered what bearing this had on the story, but she did not speak as the Lama went on:

"Hundreds of pilgrims came every year and it is believed that on this occasion her husband would always visit her."

"And she is still alive?"

"She died a few months ago," the Lama said, "but it is known only by those who know such things that her husband, Nana Sahib, died only three years ago."

"So he is dead," Chandra said. "I am glad! His was a cruel and wicked act!"

"For which he will pay the penalty in many lives," the Lama said quietly. "We can never escape from our deeds, whether they be good or bad."

For a moment he lapsed into silence, and Chandra wondered if this was the end of the story. Then he went on:

"While he was alive it was an open secret in Nepal that Nana Sahib sold the valuable jewels which he had brought with him from India to the Prime Minister, Jang Bahadur. He bought them one after another. Amongst them was an emerald seven-and-a-half centimetres long, which went into the official regalia."

The Lama's voice altered as he continued:

"These jewels were of no importance, except for one to which he is not entitled and which should be returned to where it belongs."

"And where is that?" Chandra asked, knowing the answer.

"The Sakya-Cho Monastery," the Lama answered, "where it had lain in the forehead of the Lord Buddha for a thousand years before it was stolen."

"Stolen?" she exclaimed in surprise.

"Nana Sahib had an insatiable desire for fine gems," the Lama replied. "One of his spies must have told him of our precious emerald, and then one day it was gone."

"It is what one might expect of a man like that," Chandra said scornfully, "to steal what is sacred."

"I understand he would never sell the emerald," the Lama said, "because he considered it to be lucky, but now that he is dead, it must be returned to where it belongs."

"I can understand your feelings," Chandra said; "but how can I help you?"

"When you are in Katmandu," the Lama said, "the emerald will be handed to you."

"By whom?" Chandra enquired.

"That is not for me to say, or for you to know," the Lama replied. "Sufficient that you will find it in your possession. All I ask is that, as your father's daughter, you will bring it safely to me when you cross the border back into India."

Chandra looked at him with a worried expression on her face.

"Surely if you know who has the stone, it will be easy for you to get it back?"

The Lama smiled as if she was being very stupid.

"There are always those who want jewels for their material value," he said, "and now that Nana Sahib is dead, and his wife, there will be vultures who would strip them of what is vaulable just for their own needs."

"Of course, I understand," Chandra said, "but will it be . . . dangerous for me to carry the . . . stone?"

"If you will be gracious enough to do so, you will be protected by our prayers," the Lama said, "and I do not need to tell you that where a European would be safe, the same would not apply to a Tibetan."

Chandra could understand only too well what he was saying. At the same time, she felt herself shrink from being involved in what she was quite sure was a dangerous game of theft and counter-theft.

She knew only too well that there were thieves in India who would not stop at murder to get their hands on some of the magnificent jewels belonging to the Temples or to the Maharajahs.

But the former would have Priests to guard them, and the latter would have soldiers, while she would be alone.

Then she asked herself what could be a better protection than the prayers of men who were Holy and who had spiritual powers that were not understood by those who know only the West.

She made up her mind impulsively as she said to the Lama:

"I will do as you ask, but protect me, for I feel I shall . . . need it."

"You will be protected, my daughter," the Lama said, "and the merits you will acquire will bring you the happiness you seek."

Chandra looked at him in surprise, thinking she was not conscious that she was seeking happiness in any particular sort of way.

"One thing more, my daughter: if it is possible, as I believe it will be, for you to right a wrong and to restore to us what is ours, then my Monastery will not be ungrateful and I know that what we will offer you will be of assistance to your father."

.Chandra knew that he meant money. While she would have liked to say that that was completely immaterial, she thought swiftly that anything that helped her father in the future, she would be foolish to refuse.

"Thank you," she said, "and I know that if my father were here he would thank you too."

"It is we who will thank you," the Lama said with dignity.

Feeling that the conversation was at an end, Chandra rose to her feet.

"You will pray for me?" she asked. "And pray also for Papa? He is not well, and I worry about him."

"I have told you that his time is not yet come," the Lama said. "There is still work for him to do—work which, though you do not think so, will prove of great benefit to those who have ears to hear."

Chandra put her fingers together and made the obeisance, and the Lama raised his hand and blessed her.

Then, as if he had no more to say, he closed his eyes and his fingers went to his rosary.

Just for a moment Chandra stood looking at him,

then she turned and ran back towards the Bungalow.

As she reached it, her thoughts were so full with the story that the Lama had told her and what had happened so unexpectedly that she opened the back door and walked in without thinking there was any need for secrecy.

Only as she entered the passage was she aware that coming through the other door from the verandah was Lord Frome.

He looked at her in surprise, then as she shut the back door behind her and walked towards him, he asked:

"Where have you been, Miss Wardell?"

Just for a moment she contemplated telling him the truth. Then she knew that what she had heard must be secret, completely and absolutely secret from everyone, including him.

She smiled at him and it was quite an impertinent twist of her lips.

"That, My Lord, is my business!" she said, and entered her bedroom and shut the door in his face.

Chapter Four

Chandra was up early and had finished her packing before she went to breakfast at about six o'clock.

She was surprised to find that Lord Frome had already eaten and the servant was waiting to serve her alone.

It was an English breakfast, with the small eggs which were characteristic of the East, and the bacon, which no Muslim would eat, was delicious.

There was also coffee of an excellent quality, which she guessed Lord Frome had brought with him.

As soon as she had finished she went outside and found, as she had expected, that there was a large cavalcade of ponies already loaded with their baggage and what seemed a strange assortment of boxes, guns, and many indistinguishable objects which she felt sure that Lord Frome thought were necessary to his comfort.

The thick-set, thick-necked Bhutan ponies were, as Chandra knew of old, very sure-footed.

Lord Frome, who was supervising everything, greeted her in a perfunctory manner and she had a feeling that he was slightly embarrassed, although she could not be sure.

What she noticed immediately was that his servants addressed her as "Lady Sahib," which meant he had already informed them that she was his wife.

Each of the ponies had a *syce,* of groom, in attendance, and Chandra was helped onto the one she was to ride, which to her relief had a side-saddle.

She could not help wondering how Lord Frome had managed to procure one so quickly when it was obvious that it would not have been included in his equipment before she arrived.

They started off almost at once, and the *syce* who was in charge of Chandra's pony told her they had to travel a long distance first through the forests and valleys of a lower range of hills where the road was better than it would be later.

It was a fresh morning with just a hint of snow in the air before the sun dispersed it, and Chandra was thrilled with the beauty of everything she saw.

In the books she had read with her father immediately after Lord Frome's arrival at the Manor, she had learnt that on the low and level lands of Nepal there were elephants, tigers, and rhinoceros, and in the higher parts were bears and deer of every variety.

She hoped they would not encounter any tigers, which she knew from her knowledge of India could be extremely dangerous and if they were hungry would even attack travellers.

It was, however, difficult to think of anything but the loveliness of the flowers which grew on every available piece of open ground, and the wild orchids and convolvuluses which made great patches of vivid colour as they climbed up the trees.

She remembered how Sir Brian Hodgson had catalogued the flora and fauna of Nepal and she wished now that she had had time to read his books before she had left England.

Alternatively, she would have much preferred to be with her father.

His travels in the East, especially in Tibet, had made him very knowledgeable about rare plants, and she felt certain that they were something which would not interest Lord Frome.

As soon as the path narrowed, he rode ahead rather like a Commander-in-Chief, while she followed directly behind him, with the long cavalcade of burdened ponies with His Lordship's personal servants bringing up the rear.

She was certain that he was still resenting the fact that she was there.

At the same time, although she disliked him, she could not help thinking that he was a fine-looking man, and the way he rode, even though it was only on one of the mountain-ponies, told her that he was in fact a horseman.

She realised that the long years at the Manor when they had not been able to afford to keep horses and she could only occasionally be offered a ride by one of their neighbours had got her muscles sadly out of practice.

This meant, of course, that she could expect to be very stiff after a long day's riding, and she would certainly be in what might prove to be a lamentable condition by the time they reached Katmandu.

She had therefore exercised herself very strenuously every day on board ship.

It was not the same as riding a horse, but at least she loosened up her body, and she also practised the Yoga-breathing which her father had said had helped him so enormously amongst the high mountains in Tibet.

They were quite simple breathing-exercises and yet Chandra felt that they would help her to endure what she knew would be a severe test of her strength.

She was aware of how angry and contemptuous Lord Frome would be if she collapsed. It was exactly what he would expect of a woman, and she told herself that whatever she suffered on the trip, she would never complain or let him think that she was unable to do anything that a man could do.

They had gone quite a distance before they stopped at midday for a meal. It was not a very exciting one, but Chandra was glad to rest and she was in fact thirsty.

While they had been sheltered by the trees during this part of the journey, the sun, when it percolated through them, was very strong and she was glad that she had brought with her a broad-brimmed hat to protect her face.

While they were eating their luncheon, Lord Frome being surly and monosyllabic, she noticed the butterflies hovering over the blue Himalayan poppies and primulas.

They were so beautiful that she would have liked to sketch them, as she sometimes had done when she was with her father.

But she felt that it was not something she could ask Lord Frome for permission to do. Besides, she was quite certain that he was in a hurry to move on.

When they did so, there were more wild orchids climbing up the trees than she had ever seen before.

The books she and her father had read had told her that there were six hundred species of orchids in the foothills of the Himalayas, and she wished she knew the names of those that she saw.

By the afternoon Chandra was beginning to feel very tired, but she would rather have died than admit it to the man riding ahead of her.

He had made no effort to converse with her when they had had luncheon together, and she could feel an aura of resentment emanating from him which was inescapable.

"One thing is quite obvious," she told herself, "that

I will certainly earn the six hundred pounds he gave to Papa, if only for putting up with his disagreeableness."

It was growing late in the afternoon and Chandra thought that not only was she tired but so were the ponies, when her *syce* pointed ahead.

"Síságarhi Hill," he said.

Chandra looked up to see a sharp and what appeared to be an almost impassable incline, and on the crest of it she could see what looked like a fortification.

"Stay night," the *syce* said with relish.

Twenty minutes later they started up the hill.

Chandra had been told that the road to Nepal was rough and difficult and now she knew that the description had not been exaggerated.

Although she was riding, by the time they reached the top she was as breathless as her pomy was, and when she dismounted she found herself staggering and thought her legs would not carry her.

Fortunately, Lord Frome was too preoccupied and intent to notice her as they moved into what had originally been a quite small fortified town.

There were only a few peasants living in it now and there was a Dak-Bunaglow provided for travellers. It was not as well built or as comfortable as the one at Bairagnia, but Chandra was too tired to care.

When Mehan Lall had carried in her luggage, unpacked her pillow, and arranged the padded quilt on the bed, all she wanted to do was to lie down and rest.

She was informed that her meal would be ready in half-an-hour, and she forced herself to find the sluice, which was very primitive. Having washed, she changed into the same simple gown she had worn the night before.

Lord Frome was already in the Dining-Room, if it

could be given such a pretentious name, when she entered it.

Tonight there was no table-cloth, only a rough wooden table and chairs which obviously had been made locally.

There was, however, the same choice of drinks as there had been the night before, and because she felt so tired, Chandra asked if she could have a whisky.

She thought Lord Frome raised his eye-brows, and although she hated whisky and it was something she never drank as a rule, she was too exhausted to care what he or anyone else thought of a woman asking for what was considered exclusively a man's drink.

She saw some oranges on a side-table, and because she disliked the taste of her drink, she cut one of the oranges in half and began to squeeze it into the whisky.

"The servant can do that for you," Lord Frome said.

"I can manage," Chandra answered.

"I presume, as you obviously dislike the taste of whisky, that you are drinking it because you are tired."

Lord Frome spoke as if he had scored a point over her, and she replied:

"Not entirely. As you well know, alcohol in the tropics is considered a prevention against fever and other types of disease. One could also consider it an antiseptic."

There was a faint smile on Lord Frome's lips, as if he knew that she was evading the real reason for her choice, but he said nothing more, and a servant brought in the inevitable bowl of hot soup.

The menu differed little from what it had been the night before, except, Chandra thought, the chicken was tougher.

She refused the pudding, which looked to her very much like Queen's Pudding, which she had always disliked as a child, and instead helped herself to some fruit.

"Tomorrow," Lord Frome said, breaking a long silence, "after we have crossed the valley beyond this range, we shall then ascend the Chandragiri Mountains, from which we can have an excellent view of the valley of Nepal."

"I am very much looking forward to seeing it," Chandra answered. "It seems strange that there is not an easier route into the country."

"The Nepalese find it easy enough," he replied. "They are used to carrying heavy loads on their backs. They bring in woollen goods, furs, and sheep, and I am told that when the Prime Minister wanted a grand piano, they packed it in an enormous wooden crate and it came on this same route, on the shoulders of some hundred carriers!"

"That sounds to me sheer cruelty!" Chandra exclaimed.

"They like their country to belong to them and to no-one else," Lord Frome replied, "and who shall blame them? I think everybody would like a little Eden where they can be alone."

"It would, of course, depend upon whom you shared it with," Chandra answered.

"That goes without saying," Lord Frome said coldly.

The servants left the room and he went on:

"I suppose I should have asked you if you have everything you need. If you do not, do not hesitate to tell Mehan Lall or me."

"I have everything, thank you," Chandra said. "And now, My Lord, if you will excuse me, I will go to bed and prepare myself for tomorrow."

She rose from the table as she spoke, and for a moment Lord Frome did not move. Then he said:

"I have been rather remiss in not asking you what is your Christian name. It is certainly something that, as your supposed husband, I ought to know."

"It is Chandra."

"An Indian name," Lord Frome remarked, "which I know means the 'Moon.' "

"Both my father and mother loved India," Chandra replied.

She had reached the door before Lord Frome got to his feet.

"Good-night—Chandra," he said.

There was a pause before her name and she knew that he forced himself to say it.

"Good-night, My Lord," she replied formally, but as she found her way to her bedroom she was smiling.

She had forced him into the position where he had to ask her what he wanted to know, and that, she felt, was a triumph, although a very small one.

She wondered how much longer he would keep up his aloof attitude and his resentment of the fact that she was there at all.

It would be difficult, she thought, for him not to talk to her, and in fact not to be more friendly when they were actually looking at manuscripts and discussing their merits.

"One thing is quite certain," she told herself. "He may think he is a determined and dedicated bachelor entirely through his own choice, but he would find it very difficult to find any woman who would put up with him, even though he is a Lord and doubtless very rich."

As she undressed, Chandra thought sleepily how she had always imagined that one day she would find a man whom she would love and who would love her, and they would be as happy together as her father and mother had been.

Money was not really important, although of course one did not actually want to starve.

What would be exciting in a marriage would be to have the same interests, the same ambitions.

It was extraordinary, when she thought of it, how very few young men she had met.

The visitors they had had in the last five years had all been her father's contemporaries, because, with the exception of Lord Frome, he did not know any younger men who had devoted their lives to the search for Sanskrit manuscripts and the translation of them.

It seemed strange that they should all be so old. Sir Brian Hodgson was only nineteen when he had first gone to Nepal and become interested in the un-discovered treasures with which the Monasteries abounded.

He had also begun then his interest in the flowers and plants of the country, and also the animals and birds which had never before been catalogued.

In her father's book Chandra had read one of his letters that had been published after his death, in which he said:

Zoology and the branches of birds and quadrupeds amuse me very much. I have three native artists always employed in drawing from nature. I possess a live tiger, a wild sheep, a wild goat, four bears, three civets and three score of our beautiful pheasants—a rare menagerie!"

'I want to sketch,' Chandra had thought.

Riding through the woods, she had not seen a bear or a civet but she had had a quick glimpse of several pheasants and longed to discuss with somebody their beauty.

The Himalayan pheasant was, she had always known, one of the most beautiful birds in the world.

She got into bed now and as she fell asleep she was thinking how she would like to be on this journey with somebody she loved.

Someone who would understand how the beauty of everything she saw, whether it was the flowers, the pheasants, or the trees, was etched in her mind so that she felt she could never forget it.

* * *

She felt that she had hardly closed her eyes before she was awakened by a sharp knocking on the door, and she knew it was Mehan Lall calling her.

Yawning, she began to get out of bed, only to find with dismay that she was extremely stiff.

It was quite cold and she longed at that moment for a warm bath which would ease away the aches and pains of her body.

But there was no time even to think of such things.

Quickly she put on her riding-habit, remembering that as they were going higher she might need warmer clothing than she had worn the preceding day.

There had been amongst her mother's clothes a coat lined with lambs'-wool, which Mrs. Wardell had always said was her most treasured possession when she was travelling.

Chandra pulled it from her trunk, and when she was dressed she told Mehan Lall to strap the coat to her saddle so that she could put it on when she needed it.

He nodded his head to show that he understood; then Chandra ran quickly to the room where she knew breakfast would be waiting.

As she entered, she saw, with a feeling of consternation, that Lord Frome had just finished and was in the act of rising from the table.

"You are late!" he said abruptly.

"I am sorry," Chandra said. "I rose as soon as I heard the knock on the door. But tomorrow I will ask to be called earlier."

She felt that he was not placated by her explanation, but merely said as he walked towards the door:

"We shall be leaving in four minutes!"

She thought his rudeness was insufferable and she

longed to tell him that in that case he could leave without her, but she had the uncomfortable feeling that if she did so, he might in fact leave her alone to follow as best she could.

The coffee was too hot to swallow quickly, so she was forced to leave her cup half-full, and she managed to eat only a very little before she went outside to find the whole baggage-train waiting for her and Lord Frome already mounted on his pony.

Feeling rather as if she were a school-girl who had arrived after the class had started, Chandra allowed herself to be helped into the saddle. Lord Frome rode off and she followed immediately behind him as she had done the day before.

First there was a steep descent into a small valley, and then they started to climb again.

Here the road was as bad as anything Chandra had ever known, and she could understand that the Nepalese Government considered the mountains, with their formidably steep ascents and descents, as part of the natural fortifications on which they relied to keep out unwelcome visitors.

They stopped for a midday meal and Chandra found that it was not only difficult for her to move but also very painful.

However, she was determined to say nothing, and was only glad that for the moment she could stretch herself and sit in a different position from that in which she had ridden.

They had been climbing for some time and the view below them was very beautiful, as were the mountains they could now see in the distance.

In the sunshine the peaks were not only white but seemed to turn from pink to red to gold. Chandra had heard it called the "flowering of the snows."

It was so lovely that once again she longed to have a companion with whom she could enthuse over such beauty and who would understand.

Lord Frome was still looking aloof and what she thought of as "surly," so she sat in silence, looking away from him to gaze at the view, and tried to forget that he even existed.

Even so, she felt as if he encroached upon her. He was very like a dark cloud amongst the sunshine, or, she thought, a menacing rock.

"If you have finished, I think we should be pushing on," he said so suddenly and abruptly that it made her start.

"Yes, of course," Chandra agreed.

She put on her hat, which she had taken off while they were sitting in the shade, and took a last drink of the fruit-juice which had been provided with their meal.

Then she walked rather slowly and carefully towards her pony, which was waiting for her.

The *syce* helped her into the saddle, and she thought, as she picked up the reins, that she was going to have difficulty in walking at all when they arrived where they were to stay the night.

Now it was uphill all the way, and the *syce* told her that one of the reasons they were moving away as quickly as they could from the valley was that it was easy there to catch malaria.

Chandra knew this was true and she had no wish to contract the dreaded disease which had affected her father's health and was, she was quite sure, the reason why he now had a weak heart.

Even so, she found it difficult to follow the pace at which Lord Frome was moving, and there began to be a longer and longer distance between his pony and hers.

Finally he looked back, drew his animal to a standstill, and waited until she reached him.

"You must try to keep up," he said sharply. "We still have a considerable way to go before we can stop for the night."

"I will do my best," Chandra answered, "but you must realise that the ponies are tired."

"They are used to it!" he retorted.

She knew that this was a suggestion that she was not accustomed to riding and therefore it was her fault and not that of the animal she was riding.

She was quite certain that Lord Frome was making the ride more difficult than it need be and trying deliberately to make her feel uncomfortable.

He had certainly succeeded in that, she told herself a little later, for it was now agony to go on riding, and after another hour had passed she began to feel so exhausted that she thought she might fall from the saddle.

If she did so, she would doubtless roll down the mountain and over and over on the stones until she was battered into insensibility.

She clutched the front of her saddle and forced herself to make the pony she was riding keep up with that of Lord Frome. At the same time, she was trying not to scream because her body ached in every muscle.

'I am sure Papa would have felt the same after being so inactive for so long,' she thought.

But that was no consolation, and every step her pony took over the rough stones seemed to jolt her body unbearably.

She was so exhausted that when at last her *syce* said with a note of elation in his voice: "Look, Lady Sahib!" it was difficult to understand what he was trying to say.

Then she saw ahead of her what appeared to be a small village or fortification on top of yet another steep incline.

Up, up they went, and now at last, after what seemed to be a long-drawn-out agony of time, there was the same sort of building at which they had stayed the night before, but it was even more primitive and dilapidated.

It was surrounded by several dirty huts, their roofs patched with heavy stones, in which lived a number of ragged children.

Slowly and with great difficulty Chandra dismounted and went into the Rest House.

It seemed so small that for a moment she wondered if she would have a room to herself or, as was usual in Chinese Inns, the travellers all slept together on a kind of platform.

But she found a room, which was dusty and in need of cleaning, but she was too tired to care.

She sat down on a chair which creaked beneath her weight, and did not move until Mehan Lall came in with her baggage.

He put her trunk down on the floor and unstrapped it, laid the quilt on the bed, and unpacked her pillow.

Then he went from the room, shutting the door behind him.

'I must undress and change,' Chandra thought, pulling off her hat.

Then somehow, and she did not know how it happened, everything vanished into a grey mist.

* * *

Lord Frome, having washed and changed for dinner, waited impatiently.

He was not particularly hungry, but he liked being served when he was ready, without having to consider anyone else, least of all a woman who had thrust herself on him in what he considered a quite unnecessary manner.

He drank a whisky slowly, thinking as he did so that tomorrow he would be in Katmandu and start the research in which he was so interested.

He supposed that Chandra Wardell would be of some use, but he told himself resentfully that if he had had more time, he might have been able to get hold of Professor Edmunds, who he believed, although he was not certain, was in Darjeeling.

He was not nearly as good as Barnard Wardell. At the same time, he would quite obviously be a great deal better than any woman could be.

Lord Frome's lips tightened ominously as he thought how infuriating it was to be forced not only to drag a woman with him over the mountains of Nepal, but to introduce her as his wife.

All his life he had gone out of his way to prevent his name from being connected in any way with the numerous women who had tried to marry him for his title and for his wealth.

He was well aware how easy it was for a man to be forced into marriage just because, having been linked in gossip with one particular woman, he could only do the honourable thing, which was to offer her his name.

He had made up his mind never to marry. He disliked women with a violence which affected his whole outlook on life, and he found that the easiest way to avoid being implicated with them was to have nothing to do with the whole sex.

This was made all the easier because of his deep interest in Sanskrit manuscripts, which took him to parts of the world where women were unable to go.

He enjoyed Tibet not only because of the treasures he discovered but because he did not see a woman, apart from peasants, from the time he left India to the time he returned.

Unfortunately, the Viceroy had wished to hear of his exploits, and when he visited him at Simla he had found himself lionised by just the type of man-seeking women that he most disliked.

They fawned on him, flattered him, and did everything in their power, he thought violently, to trap him. He had made his escape as soon as it was possible.

It seemed incredible, after all the trouble he had taken to get into Nepal, which had not been easy, that in his moment of triumph the whole pleasure of it should have been spoilt by Chandra's appearance in place of her father.

Lord Frome genuinely liked the Professor and appreciated his erudition, which he quite rightly considered was unequalled.

It was farcical to imagine for one moment that his daughter, so young that she looked like a school-girl, could have anything like the expertise of her father.

But it was typical of a woman's vanity for her to assert that she had that expertise.

But whatever he felt about Chandra, Lord Frome knew that he was forced, because of the difficulty of obtaining another permit for a later date, to take her with him once she had reached Bairagnia.

He had been so angry at first, when she had appeared unexpectedly and he found that the only thing he could do was to pass her off as his wife, that he very nearly abandoned the whole expedition and told her, as he wanted to do, that she could go to hell.

But Lord Frome was very obstinate in getting his own way.

If he wanted to go to Nepal then that was exactly what he intended to do, and to have everything upset by one tiresome woman was more than he could contemplate.

"I have to take her," he had told himself through gritted teeth. "I just hope to God she is of some use, although I very much doubt it."

He had not explained to Chandra the real reason why he was so insistent that she should travel as his wife.

This was because the new British Resident, Colonel Wylie, who had not been in Katmandu for long, had advised him against approaching the Monasteries with a view to inspecting their manuscripts.

Colonel Wylie had written:

I think it would be a mistake to take any further treasures of such sort from the Nepalese. Sir Brian Hodgson, as you well know, gave a great number of the Sanskrit Manuscripts both to the Royal Asiatic Society and to the India Office. I cannot help thinking that future generations will think these valuable and unique works should remain in Nepal where they belong.

Because Lord Frome had persuaded the Viceroy to overrule Colonel Wylie on this point, he was determined that he would not give the British Resident any possible excuse to complain about him personally.

To arrive in Katmandu with a young girl whom he could merely explain away as an authority on Sanskrit would, if repeated, which it would be in Viceregal circles, make him the subject of raised eye-brows.

It might also invite a polite but thinly veiled rebuke for letting down the prestige of the British aristocracy in a backward country like Nepal.

Furious at having to stoop to such a deception, but knowing that it was necessary if he was to continue his journey, Lord Frome had surrendered himself to the inevitable.

He loathed what he had to do and hated Chandra quite unreasonably because she was instrumental in what he thought was an undoubted humiliation.

As he finished the glass of whisky in his hand, Lord Frome realised that the servants were still waiting and there was no sign of Chandra.

"Tell the Lady Sahib that dinner is ready!" he ordered.

"I have knocked on her door, Lord Sahib," his personal servant replied, "but there was no answer."

Lord Frome frowned.

Was the damned woman being deliberately difficult? he asked himself. Was she keeping him waiting while she titivated herself up? Or was she too tired to come to dinner? In which case she might have the decency to say so, and he could get on with his meal.

He was about to give another order, then changed his mind and walked from the Dining-Room across the passage to Chandra's door.

He knocked sharply but there was no answer, and now, wondering if perhaps she had gone roaming as she had the night before, he lifted the latch and looked inside.

For a moment he thought no-one was there; then, to his surprise, he saw Chandra lying on the floor almost at his feet.

He looked down at her, thinking that she must have fainted, then he saw that she was asleep.

Her hands were tucked under her cheek, and with the exception of her hat, she was still wearing the things she had worn all day.

Lord Frome looked at her for a long moment, at the long lashes, dark against her pale skin, the strange colour of her hair, which waved on either side of her oval forehead, and the perfectly curved lips which seemed to have a faint smile on them.

He saw now that she was sleeping, her breath coming slowly and evenly, and he knew it was the sleep of utter exhaustion.

Bending down, he picked her up in his arms and laid her on top of the quilt on the bed, her head against the pillow.

As he moved her, she made a little murmur and seemed almost to cuddle against him as a child might do with its mother.

But she did not wake, and he knew that she was completely unconscious of anything that was happening.

When he took his arms from her he thought suddenly that she seemed very small, slight, and rather pathetic.

Because he had been hating her, she had seemed in

his mind to be a large, dominating woman determined to get her own way, standing up to him in a manner he most disliked.

But now, instead, she merely looked very young and very vulnerable.

He stared at her for a long moment; then, realising that she was still wearing her riding-boots beneath the full skirt of her habit, he pulled them slowly from her feet.

She never even stirred as he put each small foot back on the quilt.

Then he looked round.

Over a chair, where Mehan Lall had put it, was a warm blanket.

Surprisingly gently for such a big man, Lord Frome spread it over Chandra, then went from the room, closing the door quietly behind him.

* * *

Chandra awoke because there was a noise far, far away in the distance, and she wondered why it should seem so irritating and she had no wish to hear it.

Then she realised that there was someone knocking on the door, and she opened her eyes.

"What is it?" she asked, speaking in English because she was too sleepy to remember where she was.

"Five o'clock, Lady Sahib," she heard Mehan Lall say, and then she remembered where she was and what was happening.

She was in Nepal, and last night . . .

She sat up, trying to remember what had happened last night, and found that she was wearing the coat of her riding-habit and was covered with a blanket.

She could not have done that herself. She remembered feeling desperately tired and thinking that she must undress. But what had happened?

She could not remember, and as she automatically

pushed the blanket aside to get out of bed, she saw her riding-boots.

They were on the floor beside the bed.

She knew then that someone must have taken them off, someone who had lifted her onto the bed and covered her with the blanket.

But who could it have been?

She knew that Mehan Lall would never have touched her without permission.

No Indian servant would dare touch a white Mem-Sahib.

That left only one person—and it seemed too incredible to contemplate.

Because she knew that time was passing, Chandra began to undress and redress herself.

She had intended anyway today to put on a thicker habit than she had worn yesterday, knowing that they would be high at the very top of the lofty Chandragiri Pass, which was thousands of feet high and white with snow.

Her riding-habit was on the top of her trunk and she pulled it out and with it a warm scarf for her neck.

She would also want, she knew, the sheep-lined coat that had been attached to her saddle.

Only as she took off the clothes she had worn all night did she realise how stiff she still felt and how much her body ached.

"He will despise me because I collapsed," Chandra told herself. "I must appear quite ordinary this morning."

It was a tremendous effort to dress quickly, and pulling her boots on again was a superhuman task. But she managed it, and when finally she left her bedroom and went into the room where breakfast was waiting, it was to find that Lord Frome was not yet there.

Thankfully she sat down at the table and drank a

whole cup of coffee before she attempted to eat anything.

She felt it would give her strength, and also would
enable her to face him, knowing what he must be
feeling after last night.

When she heard his footsteps before he entered the
room, she felt her heart give a sudden thump in her
breast, and a feeling of shyness and uncertainty sweep
over her.

It was something she had never felt before and she
told herself it was just shame because she had collapsed through sheer physical exhaustion, but it was
in fact a defeat that should never have happened.

"Good-morning, Chandra!" Lord Frome said in a
voice that sounded less disagreeable than usual.

"Good-morning," Chandra managed to say.

"I am glad you are early," he said conversationally
as he sat down at the table. "I want you to have the
most magnificent view of Katmandu, which you will
get within an hour of leaving here."

"I am looking . . . forward to . . . seeing it."

She wondered why it was difficult to speak and why
the food she was eating seemed to stick in her throat.

She could not look at Lord Frome directly and she
was aware that his eyes rested on her face as if he re-
assured himself that she was not going to be a nui-
sance and was well enough to travel.

"Did you have a good sleep last night?" he asked.

Because she felt that he was taunting her, remind-
ing her of how ignominiously helpless she had been,
she felt the blood flood into her cheeks.

"Yes . . . thank you."

Then, because she was sure he was gloating over
her, she added:

"Thank you for . . . looking after me. I realised it
could . . . only have been you who took off my . . .
boots and . . . covered me with a . . . blanket."

"As my guest, I could hardly leave you lying on the floor all night," Lord Frome replied.

She thought he spoke drily. At the same time, she had the feeling that he was rather surprised that she should have admitted his help and thanked him for it.

They sat in silence for a moment, then Lord Frome asked:

"You feel well enough to go on?"

Chandra was so surprised at his consideration that she looked at him wide-eyed.

As if he knew what she was saying without words, he said:

"I realise now I drove you too hard yesterday. It was inevitably a tough day, but I made it worse."

"I should not have been so . . . foolish if I were not so badly out of . . . practice," Chandra said quickly. "We have not been able to afford horses for a long time."

She saw that she had astonished him.

"Not afford horses?" he repeated. "Then how do you go anywhere?"

Chandra smiled.

"We stay at home," she replied. "Papa has never wanted to do anything but work, and as I have already told you, I work with him."

Lord Frome seemed to be choosing his words as he replied:

"But surely that is a very restricting life for a young girl?"

"I have not minded because I have been with Papa," Chandra answered, "but in the days when we had more money and Mama was alive, we used to travel and that was very exciting."

"And you really have not ridden for some time until the day before yesterday?"

"Only very occasionally, when one of our neighbours was kind enough to lend me a horse."

"You are making me feel that I have been some-what brutal."

"No, please . . . it is not your fault," Chandra replied. "I told you I could do everything my father could do, but I am sure Papa would have been less tired than I was last night."

"I rather doubt that," Lord Frome said, "and I can only apologise."

She looked at him in astonishment, and then because she felt shy, she said quickly:

"I know you want to . . . start."

"You are quite certain you have had enough to eat?" Lord Frome asked. "After all, you missed a meal last night—not that it was very appetising!"

Chandra gave a little laugh.

"Soup, chicken, and caramel pudding!" she said before she could prevent herself.

"I cannot remember, but I have a suspicion that that was what it was," Lord Frome agreed, and added: "If you are ready, I think we should be on our way."

They went outside, and for the first time Lord Frome inspected Chandra's pony to see if the girths were as tight as they ought to be and if the saddle was in the right place.

Everything appeared to be in order, and when she had mounted, he swung himself onto his own pony and set off ahead.

He had been right in saying that it was a stiff climb, and when they came to the top of the hill, there in the rising sun lay the great range of the Himalayas, their peaks vivid against the blue sky, while far below them the valley was still shrouded in swirling mists.

There was a long descent, and now Chandra could see below them the gigantic terraces cut into the sides of the mountains, which were in fact rice-fields following the curving lines of the slope.

Amongst them were tiny houses, little brown huts

roofed with straw, isolated in little groups and with minute paths.

As they came lower there were numbers of carriers moving towards them, their strange gait half a walk, half a run, and carrying on their backs enormous burdens of food, spices, paprika, and Nepalese home-made paper from Katmandu into India.

There was still a long way to go, but now that they were actually in the vale of Katmandu, it seemed as if the journey was almost over and all the difficulties were behind them.

There was only a simple track to ascend and descend the slopes.

There were valleys with improvised bridges which seemed so insubstantial spanning roaring torrents hundreds of feet below that Chandra would close her eyes in alarm and just hope that her pony would carry her across to safety.

It grew warmer and warmer and she soon discarded her sheepskin-lined coat and considered taking off her riding-jacket.

She had read in her father's books that although Nepal was referred to as a Himalayan land and the Roof of the World, it had an ideal climate, and as she saw more and more beauty round her, Chandra began to think that Lord Frome was right in referring to it as a "little Eden."

It was afternoon before they reached Katmandu, and she realised it was in fact a city of Palaces and Temples.

It seemed impossible that so many beautiful buildings could be clustered together in one small place, and the Nepalese people themselves added to the fairy-tale feeling.

The men wore their curved knives, the *Khukri,* at their waists. The women had full skirts, long black hair in which they wore large red or yellow flowers,

and festooned their arms and necks with many ornaments of different coloured glass.

They also had a hanging gold ring in the nose and a
dozen small bronze rings at the edge of each ear.

"It is a beautiful place, full of beautiful people!"
Chandra exclaimed aloud, and Lord Frome, who was
only a few paces ahead of her, turned his head.

"We have managed to get into Eden," he remarked
in a dry voice. "Let us hope there is not an angel with
a flaming sword waiting to turn us out."

"Indeed I hope not!" Chandra cried.

She stared with delight at a huge statue in the centre
of the Square of Kala Bhairab, "The Terrible Black
One" with a severed head in his hand, trampling on a
newly conquered demon.

They rode on until they came to the Residency
where Chandra gathered they were to stay.

As soon as she saw it, she was not surprised that
Lord Frome felt he must be respectable, for it was a
very spacious and imposing edifice, in the Indian
Gothic style, with castellated edges to the roofs and a
pointed turret at each corner.

The huge Gothic windows were reminiscent of a
Cathedral, and when they entered through the huge
oak door Chandra almost expected to find an atmosphere of sanctity inside.

Colonel Wylie was a genial man who seemed delighted to welcome Lord Frome. Although he was obviously surprised to learn that he was married and had
brought his wife with him, he was too polite to say so.

Chandra was taken up to a large and impressive
bedroom but she could do nothing but run to the window to stare out at the view of the city and beyond it
at the Himalayas.

"I am here!" she told herself. "I am here, and I
thought it would be impossible that my plan would
succeed!"

She felt a prayer of gratitude rise within her because

not only had she reached Nepal but now her father would be able to get well in the warm climate of Cannes.

She knew too that ever since the Lama had told her that her father had many years of work in front of him, her anxiety on his account had gone.

Some people might think it absurd that she could believe so easily what had been said to her by a man she had never seen before but who she had been told was holy.

But Chandra had known Saddhus and Gurus in India, and though some of them were fakes, she had grown to know instinctively when one of them was genuinely dedicated to a life of prayer.

She knew she could not have been mistaken in what she felt radiating from the Lama, and she knew too that when he had said he would pray for her and she would be protected, he had been talking in all seriousness.

At the same time, now that she was in Katmandu, she felt slightly afraid of her own involvement with the emerald that Nana Sahib had stolen.

Such jewels were too notorious for there not to be a great number of people who knew about them.

How was it possible that perhaps one of the most valuable of them all, the emerald that had come from the Monastery at Sakya-Cho, could be entrusted to her and no-one be aware of it?

Chandra was sensible enough to be aware that if it was known that she was carrying it out of the country, her life would not be worth the flick of a coin.

Then as she felt a little tremor of fear inside her, she looked at the far-distant peaks of the Himalayas and told herself that she was only a very small part of the wheel of life,—the wheel in which everything has its place and every deed its reward or retribution.

It was only right that the Monastery should have back their precious stone which to them was sacred, and if in helping them she could undo some of the wrong that Nana Sahib had done, then she should feel privileged by the opportunity.

"I will not be afraid," Chandra said to herself.

At the same time, she felt helpless and alone in a strange country, while her father, the only person she really loved, was thousands and thousands of miles away.

Chapter Five

The Nepalese maid suggested to Chandra that she should rest while she unpacked in another room.

Thankful to be able to do so, because she was still aching from the long ride, Chandra got into bed and almost immediately fell asleep.

She awoke with a start because someone was speaking to her, and she found her maid trying to tell her that her bath was ready and it was time for her to dress for dinner.

She felt, as she awoke, that she had come back from a long, long distance, and she wanted more than anything else to turn over and go on sleeping.

But she knew that however fatigued she might be, she must appear at dinner and play the part of Lord Frome's wife.

She realised that near her bedroom was a bathroom, which was a modern innovation she had not expected to find in Nepal, and she wondered if it had been added in the Residency by Sir Brian Hodgson or the Resident who came after him.

Whoever had built it, it was a joy to soak in hot water scented with lotus-blossom and to feel a little of her stiffness begin to ebb away.

Nevertheless, as she dried herself she realised that she was very tired, and she hoped that she would be able to retire early and have a good night's sleep before starting the real work on the object of their journey.

She was looking forward not only to seeing the Sanskrit manuscripts and the Monastery in which they were located, but also to showing Lord Frome that she was not as useless as he thought she would be.

She could not help feeling that she had "lost face," as they would say in the Orient, because she had collapsed last night.

At the same time, she told herself proudly, she had not hindered him or delayed their arrival in Katmandu, which she might easily have done.

He could not really complain of her, although she was quite certain that he was still resenting the fact that she was a woman rather than a man.

Having finished her bath, she went into the bedroom to find her maid laying out on an arm-chair the gown she was to wear this evening.

Only as she saw it did Chandra realise that, being so tired, she had forgotten to ask the maid to press it.

In consequence, having remained packed since she had left the ship, it was creased and looked even more shabby than it was already.

She explained to the maid what she wanted, and the Nepalese girl smiled as she hurried from the room, carrying the gown over her arm.

Wrapped in her plain wool dressing-gown, with her hair hanging over her shoulders, Chandra went to the window and was once again irresistibly drawn by the view of the city.

Now the peaks of the Himalayas were shrouded in clouds and she knew she would have to wait until dawn to see them again in all their glory.

There was a knock on the door, and, thinking that

the maid had returned very quickly, Chandra automatically said: "Come in!"

Then, to her surprise, it was not the door to the passage which opened but one she had not noticed before. Now as Lord Frome entered she knew it must communicate with the bedroom next door.

He was already dressed in his evening-clothes and they were different from those he had worn on the journey.

Now with a stiff, snowy-white shirt-front and several glittering decorations on his long-tailed evening-coat, he looked magnificent and, Chandra had to admit, even more awe-inspiring than usual.

She was surprised to see him in her bedroom and her eyes were questioning as she turned to face him.

He glanced round as if to see whether they were alone, and then he said:

"I thought I ought to warn you before you go downstairs that Colonel Wylie questioned me as to when we were married."

It was quite obvious from the way he spoke how much he disliked having to reply to the Resident's questions, and he went on:

"I told him that the ceremony took place just before I left England, and as I had not yet had time to inform all my relations or the Viceroy, I would be grateful if he would not mention it in his letters. He has promised not to do so."

He waited for her answer and Chandra replied:

"I will . . . remember what you . . . said."

Lord Frome turned as if he would leave, then as he reached the door which joined their rooms together he said:

"A party is being given for us tonight, and as the Nepalese are very colourful and bejewelled on such occasions, I suggest you wear your best gown."

He spoke casually, as if it were of no interest to him, and quite suddenly Chandra felt her temper rising.

It was not only because of the manner in which he spoke, it was also because, woman-like, she realised how she would look not only beside the Nepalese but also beside the man who was supposed to be her husband.

"My best gown!" she repeated. "How do you expect, My Lord, the impoverished daughter of a man whose life's work is to translate Sanskrit manuscripts to be able to afford a new gown of any sort?"

She spoke aggressively, and seeing the surprise in Lord Frome's eyes, she continued, her voice rising a little:

"Has it never struck you that my father, who you say is the greatest in his field, has difficulty in existing on the pittance he receives for his work on the manuscripts on which you set so much store?"

Because she was tired, the self-control she had exercised ever since she had met Lord Frome, in speaking humbly and concealing her resentment of his rudeness, broke and Chandra threw caution to the winds.

"Perhaps now that I have reached Nepal I should tell Your Lordship the truth. I came on this journey because the only way I could save my father's life was to keep the money you had given him and send him to the South of France for the winter."

There was no doubting now that Lord Frome was completely astonished by her attack, but Chandra continued:

"He was so ill not only because his heart was affected but because he did not have the right food to eat! No man could be well and live as we have these past six months on very little except eggs and the vegetables we have grown in the garden."

She drew a deep breath.

"We could barely afford bread, let alone meat, because we could not pay the trades-people, and the day you called to see my father I was wondering what was

left in the house that we could sell, so that we could
... purchase enough to keep us ... alive."

Her voice broke on the last word and she turned
away to the window to add bitterly:

"I will come down to dinner wearing a gown that
my mother made for herself eight years ago and which
was altered to fit me after she died. I have worn it for
three years. It is shabby and old and looks it!"

She paused to add defiantly:

"If you are ashamed of your 'wife's' appearance, I
am sure you can think up some plausible falsehood to
explain why I do you no credit."

She ceased speaking, her breath coming quickly
from between her lips, her heart thumping with the
intensity with which she had spoken.

Then, as she expected Lord Frome to reply, she
heard the communicating-door shut and knew he had
gone.

There were tears of anger in her eyes and as they
ran down her cheeks Chandra wiped them away
fiercely.

"I told him the truth," she said. "If he does not like
it, there is nothing he can do about it. He is so self-
centred that I do not suppose he realises there is anyone else in the world except himself."

She sat down at the dressing-table and started to
arrange her hair.

A feminine instinct made her try to do her best to
make it appear fashionable.

There was no point now in appearing studious as
she had tried to do when she had first met Lord
Frome.

Instead, she piled her hair on top of her head and
told herself that since the Nepalese would expect an
Englishwoman to look strange in their eyes, the only
person likely to be really critical of her appearance
was Colonel Wylie.

She had just finished arranging her hair when the maid came back into the room with her gown.

It certainly looked better than it had when it had been taken from her trunk.

Chandra put it on, and although the white silk of which it was made had turned ivory with age and the inexpensive lace which edged the low neck had not the crispness that it had had when it was new, the tight bodice revealed her perfectly proportioned figure and her waist was fashionably tiny above the full skirt.

However, woman-like, she looked at herself critically and could see only that the gown was nearly threadbare at the seams and was certainly not fashionable enough to complement the magnificence of Lord Frome, resplendent with his decorations.

There was a knock on the door and the maid went to answer it. When she came back she carried on a silver salver two sprays of orchids and a glass of champagne.

Chandra stared at them in surprise, then told herself that Lord Frome was apologising in quite a practical manner.

She did not feel elated, as if she had scored off him, but because she was tired she felt strangely near to tears.

She took a sip of the champagne, then picked up one of the long sprays of orchids and held it up to her head.

The Nepalese maid gave an exclamation and took it from her.

Deftly she arranged the orchids not on the top of Chandra's head but at the back, as the Indian women wore them, and Chandra realised at once that this was exactly the right place.

They looked very pretty, seeming to fall from the crown of her head to the base of her neck, and when she picked up the second spray she knew that she should pin it at her waist.

The flowers certainly made a difference, and when she had drunk the rest of the champagne she told herself she could now go downstairs with confidence and not feel as shabby and insignificant as she had felt before.

Even so, it was an ordeal to descend the wide staircase, which might have come straight from some Scottish Baronial Castle.

A servant in a white and red uniform led her across the marble hall.

There was a chatter of voices as he showed Chandra into the Reception-Room, and she felt almost as if she had stepped into the parrot-house of some exotic Zoo.

The spacious room with its carved ceiling and imposing portraits of previous Residents seemed to be filled with so much colour and glitter that for a moment Chandra felt bewildered.

Then she realised that the Resident's guests were all arrayed in the most brilliant hues. There were not only the women's sari-like gowns, but also the men's uniforms were colourful, while their decorations rivalled their wives' jewels.

Never had Chandra seen so many huge emeralds, rubies, diamonds, and every other sort of stone worn not only round the neck and wrists but in the nose, the ears, and on the dark, almost jet-black hair of the Nepalese ladies.

She could understand only too clearly why Lord Frome had advised her to wear her best gown, and for just one moment she wanted to run away from these glittering, colourful people and hide herself upstairs.

Then the Resident was beside her and introduced her first to the Prime Minister and his wife, and then to the rest of his guests, all of whom had important titles and long, almost unpronounceable names.

But that was the only stiff or difficult thing about them.

The dark eyes of the Nepalese glittered, their lips smiled, and they chattered away excitedly, delighted to find that Chandra understood their own language and was able to reply in the same tongue.

There were only a few instances when someone more fluent in both languages was obliged to translate the exact meaning of a sentence.

By the time they sat down to dinner, which was served in what Chandra thought was semi-Regal style, with a *Khitmutgar* behind every chair, she had forgotten all about her appearance and was enjoying herself because it was such a different party from any she had ever been to before.

She had not dared to look for Lord Frome when she came into the Reception-Room, and only when she was seated at the table, the Prime Minister on one side of her and a General of the Gurkhas on the other, did she steal a glance at him.

She saw that he was being unexpectedly genial to a Nepalese lady on his right.

He was laughing at something she had said and it made him look very much more handsome and much younger.

'What a pity he cannot always be like that,' Chandra thought to herself, and wondered a little apprehensively if he was very angry at the way she had raged at him in her bedroom.

She told herself that she had behaved badly, and however rude Lord Frome might have been on the journey, that was no excuse for her to be rude too.

After all, she was beholden to him for six hundred pounds, the money that would make her father well, and for that at least she should show her gratitude.

'I must apologise,' she thought.

It was impossible for Chandra ever to bear a grudge for long or really to dislike anyone, however difficult

they might be; and having what her father might have
called "let off steam," her resentment and what at
first had seemed to be a positive dislike of Lord Frome
had vanished.

She found herself feeling ashamed of the way she
had behaved and finding every excuse for his behaviour on the journey.

She could understand that, being so proud, he must
at this moment be loathing the pretence that she was
his wife and having to lie to the Resident.

Yet, instead of being understanding and sympathetic,
she had merely vented her rage upon him, simply, she
told herself, because he had "touched her on the raw."

No woman, young or old, however intelligent she
might be, could fail to be depressed at never having
a new gown, never being able to wear anything but
what Ellen often referred to as "your old rags."

Although Chandra had progressed from her own
clothes, which had grown too tight for her, into her
mother's, she never wore anything she had chosen
for herself.

Any money her mother had expended on clothes
went on the riding-habits she needed for travelling and
for the other garments which were essential if she was
to accompany her husband on his journeys, which took
him from the burning heat of the plains into the icy-
cold regions of snow.

The pretty gowns which she had when they settled
down in the country she had made herself, with the
help of Ellen, and though they were exquisitely
stitched, the material had been cheap and many of
the dresses had literally fallen to bits after Chandra
had worn them for several years.

She had told herself that clothes were unimportant
and that it was what was in the mind that counted.

But when she had gone to Church on Sundays and
had seen the girls of her own age who were merely
the daughters of the local farmers wearing far more

fashionable and attractive clothes than she could ever afford, it had been hard not to feel a little envious, and she had longed for something new, even if it was only a rose to put on her hat.

But if it was a question between food and raiment, Ellen made quite certain that any money they had was spent on the former.

"How can I expect somebody like Lord Frome to understand?" Chandra asked herself. "He is rich. He has always had everything he ever wanted in life. How could he have any idea how difficult it is to make ends meet when there is simply not enough money coming into the house?"

However, Chandra did not want to let her guilty feelings over losing her temper spoil the evening, so she forced herself to laugh and talk to the Nepalese gentlemen sitting on either side of her.

When the ladies retired to the Drawing-Room it was a joy to talk to the soft-voiced women and inevitably to admire their jewellery.

The emeralds which so many of them wore made her think of the emerald she was to carry from Nepal back to India, and she felt a sudden pang of fear in case anyone should ever guess that such an important stone was in her possession.

She had longed, during dinner, to ask the Prime Minister if she could see Nana Sahib's emerald, which the Lama had said was seven-and-a-half centimetres long and which was in the official regalia.

Then she told herself that even to admit that she had ever heard of Nana Sahib might be a mistake.

She began to feel as if she was part of a drama that might develop into terror and danger, simply because already she was inhibited from speaking of one man and was apprehensive of something which might happen in the future.

The Nepalese ladies chattered away gaily, inviting Chandra to their Palaces and telling her proudly of the

European pieces of furniture and other luxuries which had been brought to them over the same road by which she had entered Nepal.

Soon after the gentlemen joined the ladies in the Drawing-Room, the Prime Minister was ready to make his farewells, and immediately, as if at a signal, all the other guests began leaving.

It was still quite early in the evening, but the Resident explained that most Nepalese started their day at dawn, so they seldom stayed out late at night.

"That is a great relief to us," Lord Frome said before Chandra could speak, "because my wife and I will have to start very early to reach the Monastery."

The Resident gave him a quick glance, as if he was questioning the wisdom of searching for manuscripts after his letter on the subject, but he said nothing and Lord Frome went on:

"We too will say good-night, and thank you for a most delightful party. I thought the Prime Minister a very charming man."

"Bir Sham Shir is a moderate and progressive ruler," Colonel Wylie replied, "and his capacity for enjoyment exceeds that of his predecessors."

"He was telling me tonight," Lord Frome said, "that he is building a swimming-bath in one of his Palaces. That certainly seems a strange innovation, especially in this part of the world."

The Resident laughed.

"I think he is obsessed with water. In another Palace, which is surrounded by a circular canal, he has leaping fountains that are illuminated with coloured lights in the evenings."

Chandra gave an exclamation.

"Now I understand," she said, "what the Prime Minister's wife meant when she asked me if I would like to see the coloured lights! It must be very attractive!"

"We must certainly see that you accept that invitation, Lady Frome," the Resident said. "And may I tell you what a success you were this evening? As my guests said their good-byes they all paid you the most extravagant compliments."

Chandra's eyes widened, then she blushed.

"Thank . . . you," she said in a low voice.

"I hope you will have the chance of meeting a great many more Nepalese while you are here," the Resident went on. "I am sure you will be inundated with invitations when those who met you tonight sing your praises in Katmandu."

"You are making me feel . . . embarrassed," Chandra murmured.

As she spoke, she looked at Lord Frome from under her eye-lashes, wondering if he was pleased with or indifferent to the fact that she had obviously been a success.

However, he was moving towards the door and she knew that he was anxious to retire.

She would have liked to go on listening to more compliments about herself, for they were something she had very seldom heard, but, knowing what was expected of her, she put out her hand.

"Good-night, Your Excellency," she said to the Resident, "and thank you very, very much for the most wonderful party I have ever attended."

She spoke with a sincerity that was unmistakable and the Resident was obviously delighted.

Then Chandra hurried after Lord Frome.

They walked up the wide staircase together, and as he opened the door of her room for her he said:

"Good-night, Chandra."

"Good-night, My Lord, and thank you very much for the orchids!"

"They became you," he replied, then shut the door.

It was another compliment, even if a very small one, from the man who was pretending to be her husband, and Chandra felt that she should have taken the opportunity to apologise for her behaviour earlier in the evening.

But Lord Frome had shut the door on her as he spoke, and she wondered if he had been afraid that she might continue to rage at him.

All men hated a scene, which was undoubtedly what she had caused, and she should, as Ellen would have said, "feel thoroughly ashamed of herself."

On an impulse, without really thinking, Chandra walked across the room and knocked on the communicating-door to Lord Frome's bedroom.

For a moment there was no answer, but then with what was obviously a note of surprise in his voice he said:

"Come in!"

She went in to find him standing in front of a chest-of-drawers above which was a mirror.

She realised that he was taking his wallet out of the pocket of his tail-coat, and he turned to face her with what she thought was a question in his eyes.

Quickly, because she felt shy, she said, hurrying over her words:

"I . . . I just wanted to say I am . . . sorry I was rude before dinner. Please . . . forgive me. I have no excuse for behaving as I did . . . except that I was . . . tired."

Lord Frome walked towards her.

"I understand that, but I did not understand that your father was living in such difficult conditions."

"There is no reason why you should . . . concern yourself with . . . us," Chandra said humbly, "except that Papa is . . . useful to you."

"Very useful," Lord Frome said; "but, though I realised that scholars are lamentably under-paid, I imagined, if I thought of it at all, that your father had an income of his own."

"Papa receives a pension of seventy pounds a year from the Bengal Asiatic Society," Chandra replied,

"and last year you paid him one hundred fifty pounds
for the two manuscripts he translated for you."

"Is that all he had?" Lord Frome enquired.

"There was about twenty pounds in royalties from
previous books, and he wrote some articles which
brought in five pounds. The magazines which publish
such things have a very small circulation."

Lord Frome's lips tightened.

"I should have realised all this before," he said, "but
quite frankly, it never struck me that scholars of your
father's reputation should not be more appreciated
financially."

"Papa has a most imposing list of distinctions from
a great numer of different countries," Chandra said.
"Unfortunately, we cannot eat them!"

"I am beginning to realise that," Lord Frome said,
"and really, Chandra, I am appalled by what you have
told me."

"Everything is all right for the moment," Chandra
said, almost as if she was reassuring him. "Thanks
to the money you gave Papa, he has been able to
go to a small Pension at Cannes, with Ellen to look
after him. If he spends the winter there, I am sure he
will be well by the time I return home."

"And what do you expect to happen then?" Lord
Frome asked.

The answer, Chandra knew, was that she hoped to
receive the further six hundred pounds that he had
promised her father.

But then she told herself that perhaps because she
had taken his place, Lord Frome would not think
that she was worth the same money as if she had been
a man.

Anyway, it was impossible to put her hopes into
words, and instead she said:

"I expect . . . something will . . . turn up. The gods
have been kind up to now. If we find the Lotus Man-

uscript, there could not be a better tonic as far as Papa is concerned."

She smiled as she spoke, but there was no answering smile on Lord Frome's face.

Instead he said:

"I think sometime you and I must have a serious talk about your father's future, but not tonight."

"No, not tonight," Chandra agreed quickly.

"Go to bed," Lord Frome said, "and remember only that you were a great success with the Nepalese and that tomorrow we may find the Lotus Manuscript."

He smiled at her as he spoke and she smiled back.

Then, as if something unaccountable, to which she could not put a name, made her feel shy, she moved quickly back towards her own room.

"Good-night, My Lord," she said, "and I am sorry . . . very, very sorry I behaved so . . . badly."

As she shut the door she thought that her last words had sounded rather childish.

Then she told herself that however angry he might have been, she was sure that by now Lord Frome had forgiven her and was thinking not of her bad behaviour but of her father.

"And so he should be!" she tried to tell herself defiantly as she undressed.

But somehow the fire had gone from her feelings towards Lord Frome.

Instead, as she got into bed she found herself wondering who had broken his heart, and why, with all the opportunities that must be open to him, he had not found someone beautiful enough to repair it.

* * *

It seemed to Chandra that she had barely fallen asleep before it was morning and the maid was drawing back the curtains in her room.

But a feeling of excitement swept away the drowsiness, and despite the fact that it gave her some twinges

of pain in her stiff limbs, she jumped out of bed and
ran to the window.

Just as she expected, the sun on the mountains was
even more beautiful that it had been before.

The mountain-peaks were vivid against the blue
sky, but beneath them were white clouds hiding all
but the very tips of the long range which seemed almost to encircle the valley.

It was like a sea of clouds, and as Chandra watched,
the sun began to pick out one peak after another, turning it from white to pink and from pink to gold.

It was so lovely that she stood for a long time just
staring, feeling as if she were moving through the
clouds themselves and into the sun, which was the
spiritual light of the gods.

Then with a start she remembered what lay in front
of her, and she felt afraid not only of keeping Lord
Frome waiting, but of missing one moment when she
might be looking for the precious manuscripts.

She thought it was going to be hot, so she put on the
coolest of her mother's full-skirted riding-habits, with
only a light lawn blouse beneath it.

Then she ran downstairs to find Lord Frome eating
breakfast in a smaller room than the one in which
they had dined the night before.

The windows were opened onto the garden and
through them Chandra could see beds filled with
flowers and orchids in every colour, and those that
had been cultivated were larger than the ones she had
seen in the forest.

There were also camelias, rhododendrons, and a
mass of other familiar flowers all growing in almost
tropical profusion.

"It is so lovely!" Chandra exclaimed.

Then she realised that Lord Frome, who had risen
when she entered the room, was waiting for her to sit
down at the table.

"I will not be long," she said quickly. "Am I late?"

"No," he replied. "You have ten minutes in which to eat your breakfast before the ponies will be at the front door."

"Have we far to go?" Chandra enquired, helping herself from the dish that the servant was handing her.

"I think it is about five miles outside Katmandu," Lord Frome replied, "but it is uphill, as the Monastery is built on the side of a mountain."

"Do you think," Chandra asked in a low voice, "that as I am a woman I will be unable to go in?"

For the first time it had struck her that she might be excluded from searching for the manuscripts, although she knew that many Buddhist Monasteries allowed women from the Convents that were attached to them into all but the most secret parts of the building.

"I have already made enquires about that," Lord Frome said, "and although you will not be allowed to enter the part of the Monastery where the Monks live, you will be allowed into the Library."

"Thank goodness for that!" Chandra exclaimed. "I had a sudden fear that I would be shut out, but I am sure Papa would have known if that was likely to happen."

"You will be admitted," Lord Frome repeated, "and I shall be able to see if you are as proficient as you tell me you are in recognising the ages and sources of the manuscripts we shall find there."

It was what Chandra might have expected him to say, but somehow the words did not sound pompous or even frightening.

Instead, it was almost as if he was teasing her, and she looked up from her plate to find that he had a twinkle in his eyes.

"I might as well inform you," he said, "that you do not look in the least like a blue-stocking—the sort of women who have always frightened me!"

Chandra laughed.

"I do not think you could be afraid of anything," she answered, "but quite frankly, I am terrified in case I fail you . . . if the Lotus Manuscript is right under my nose, and I fail to recognise it!"

"You sounded very much more confident when you were in Bairagnia than you do here!" Lord Frome remarked.

Again he appeared to be teasing and there was a faint smile on his lips.

"I can only say," Chandra retorted, "that the 'proof of the pudding is in the eating'; and as I have finished my breakfast, My Lord, I am ready to start on our voyage of discovery."

"That is the right word for it!" Lord Frome exclaimed.

Later, as they were riding through the town, he said:

"I have a feeling that the reason why we did not see our host this morning is because he does not approve of what we are doing."

"Does not approve?" Chandra questioned.

"The Resident contends that enough manuscripts have already left Nepal, and I am therefore going to suggest to you that whatever discoveries we make, we keep them to ourselves and do not share them with him."

"Certainly not, if that is how he feels!" Chandra said indignantly. Then she added anxiously:

"Can he stop us from removing the manuscripts when we find the ones we want?"

Lord Frome shook his head.

"No; that matter will be entirely between myself and the Abbot, and as most Monasteries are in need of funds, I see no difficulty on that score."

Chandra gave a sigh of relief before she said:

"It would be too awful to find the Lotus Manuscript and then to be told that we cannot have it and must go home empty-handed."

"I feel certain we shall not do that," Lord Frome answered. "Even if the Lotus Manuscript is not there, I am sure, from what I have heard, that there will be other manuscripts of tremendous interest, so long as you can recognise them."

Chandra drew in her breath.

"You are making me nervous, and I wish more than ever that Papa were here with us."

"If he were, I imagine you would be at home," Lord Frome replied.

She thought a little wryly that it was typical of him to make everything sound practical and down-to-earth.

They were riding through Katmandu as they talked, and Chandra was thrilled with the pagoda-shaped Temples which seemed to outnumber the houses.

After passing several magnificent white Palaces, they left the city behind and were riding on a rough, narrow road with draining-ditches on each side of it.

As they continually passed peasants who were bringing in loads of wood on their backs or carrying round baskets of vegetables on the ends of bamboo poles held over their shoulders, Chandra and Lord Frome were forced to ride single-file, without conversing.

Soon they reached the foot of the mountains and as they began to climb they passed dozens of *Chaityas*, some big, some small, and always surrounded by people turning the prayer-wheels outside them.

Finally they began to climb higher and higher, up an almost perpendicular path, until above them on the side of the mountain Chandra could see the Monastery itself.

It was exactly like the Monasteries which her father had told her he had visited in Tibet, and she felt herself thrill with excitement as they drew nearer to what was a very large building fitted into the rock of the mountainside like a tooth into its socket.

It soared upwards, gaunt and many-windowed, and it seemed almost supernatural that it remained where it was and did not crumble and fall into the deep valley beneath it.

The path wound backwards and forwards, and just as Chandra felt that they must have reached their goal, she was startled by a great roar which seemed to echo and re-echo amongst the mountains themselves.

Even as she heard it she knew that it was a welcome from the six-foot-long brass trumpets with which every Monastery greeted its guests.

As they reached the gate she saw a number of Monks waiting to meet them.

As they dismounted from their ponies, an elderly Lama—whom they recognised because he wore a pointed hood with lappets falling over his shoulders, while the Monks were bare-headed—accepted a silk scarf from Lord Frome.

This, Chandra knew, was like a visiting-card in the countries round the Himalayas.

The Lama then led the way inside the building, and Chandra was aware that the Monks looked at her out of the corners of their slanting eyes.

There was a passage which seemed almost like a tunnel, then a door was opened into a room which had a huge window overlooking the valley from which they had come.

But for the moment Chandra had eyes only for the shelves with which the room was furnished.

Here, she knew from her father's description, were the manuscripts they sought, and she could see them wrapped, as she had expected, in faded silks, or some in the Chinese manner enclosed in narrow, exquisitely made boxes.

She stood looking round her with delight while Lord Frome conversed with the Lama in his own language, both using flowery sentences which sounded like the most exquisite poetry.

There was a long table of rosewood down the centre of the room and two chairs carved with curiously symbolic figures set beside it.

Finally the Lama bowed to Lord Frome, then to Chandra, and withdrew.

As the door closed behind him, Chandra with her eyes shining exclaimed:

"We are here! And look at the treasures all round us! I never imagined ... I never believed I would actually see a Library exactly as Papa described it to me!"

Lord Frome also looked round, then he asked:

"Where do we start?"

"I do not not think it matters," Chandra answered. "You take that side of the room and I will take this, and we will see what we find."

It was like the sort of treasure-hunt she had played as a child, but more exciting and more thrilling than she could possibly have imagined.

Every manuscript she took from its beautiful silk wrapping seemed a treasure of huge value, until she found that quite a number of them were in fact comparatively recent.

They were dated in the Sanskrit manner, which she translated to Lord Frome.

"*Ratna Pariksha,*" she said, when they had been working for about twenty minutes. "It is dated *Samvat 764,* which is A.D. 1644. Do you want it?"

"Of course," he answered. "I found nothing as old as that in the last Library I visited."

"I think it has thirty-five leaves."

As she spoke, Chandra wrapped the manuscript up as she had found it, then put it down on the table.

"It is a treatise on gems and precious stones," she said, "but I expect you realised that."

Lord Frome smiled, then answered:

"To be honest, I did not!"

"Perhaps when I translate it I shall enjoy it more than you will," she said with a smile.

She opened a great number of other manuscripts finding one dated 1814, but all the others were more recent.

Then she gave a little exclamation.

"Here is something very unusual which I think will excite you."

"What is it?" Lord Frome asked, coming round to her side of the table.

"It is a treatise in *Slokas* of various subjects connected with cooking and eating," she answered. "It is written on palm-leaves, and is dated *Samvat 484*."

"Are you sure?" Lord Frome enquired.

"Quite sure!" Chandra answered. "And A.D. 1364 is very early for such a work."

"Very early indeed!" he agreed. "That is something I must certainly buy!"

Chandra turned over the palm-leaves very, very carefully.

There were only six lines to a page, but she could see that with an accurate translation, which she knew would take some time, it was extremely interesting.

They went back to work, stopping only at midday to eat a meal that Lord Frome had had brought to them by his servants on ponies.

Mehan Lall brought it into the Library and laid a place for them at the end of the long table on which they were working.

Although Chandra had first thought it was a waste of precious time, she enjoyed the dishes that had been skilfully cooked at the Residency, and the wine was delicious.

It had, Lord Frome told her, been made from grapes grown in the valley.

They ate quickly, waited on by Mehan Lall. Then

as the Indian servant cleared away everything, they were back again examining the manuscripts.

They found that a great number were quite worthless, but Chandra discovered one more which Lord Frome was determined to buy.

Only when he said it was time to go back to the Residency did Chandra realise how little impact they had made so far on the thousands of manuscripts which filled the shelves from floor to ceiling.

Right up at the very top, which could be reached only by a long ladder, she could see fascinating little bunches of faded silk and she felt quite certain that each contained a masterpiece.

And yet it was likely to take them months and months to examine everything.

They rode away from the Monastery having been seen off by one of the Lamas, and Chandra noticed that Lord Frome made them a gift which was received with obvious delight.

In return they each accepted a little silk scarf printed with a prayer.

It was not until they had climbed down the winding path, which seemed more frightening going down that it had going up, that Chandra had time to read hers.

Then she said:

"This is a prayer that I shall not only find happiness but be fertile for my husband. I am surprised that the Monks should have anything so secular in their possession."

"They would have painted it after they had seen you," Lord Frome said.

"Of course!" Chandra exclaimed. "How silly I am! I never thought of that!"

"As they believe you to be my wife," Lord Frome went on, "they would obviously expect that your one amibition would be to supply me with a large number of healthy sons."

He spoke quite drily and impersonally, but Chandra, to her annoyance, found the colour rising in her face.

She hoped that he would not notice, and as there were a number of people on the road, they were once again obliged to ride single-file, so there was no chance of any further conversation.

As they arrived back at the Residency, Chandra realised that despite the fact that she had taken very little exercise compared with the other days, she was in fact quite tired.

"I think you should rest before dinner," Lord Frome said. "Thank you for your hard work today. You will find something in your bedroom which I hope you will like and accept."

Chandra looked at him in surprise, but there were servants all round them and she did not like to ask or answer questions.

Instead, she went up to her bedroom, and found as she entered it that there were a number of things laid out on the bed.

She looked at them in astonishment, for a moment not realising what they were. Then she saw that they were saris, exquisite Indian saris, embroidered with gold and silver thread, each one with a little short-sleeved blouse to match it such as Indian women wear.

For a moment Chandra stared, incredulous. Then she realised that this was Lord Frome's answer to her complaint that she had only one gown.

At first she thought it would be impossible to accept such presents from him and in fact ought not to do so.

Then she told herself that he was not thinking only of her but of himself, and if she was well dressed it would reflect on him as her husband.

She lay down but found it difficult to sleep because she was so eager to see herself in one of the saris.

Long ago she had learnt how to wear one correctly,

when she and her mother had been in India together.

It had amused them, in the evenings when they were alone with her father, to dress up as if they were Indian women and to have dinner with him with flowers in their hair, wearing round their wrists the cheap bangles that could be bought in any native Bazaar.

When Chandra had had her bath she put on a silk sari of the most exquisite shade of pink, embroidered with silver.

She knew it was a very expensive garment, and once again she felt a little qualm in case she should not have allowed Lord Frome to spend so much money on her.

Then she told herself that it would be needlessly rude and very prudish to refuse his generosity.

After all, if she could pretend to be his wife, it was certainly "straining at a gnat and swallowing a camel" to say that she was too conventional to accept a present.

The bodice fitted her well, and she pleated the sari round her waist and fastened it at the front, then flung over her left shoulder what was left of the conventional five yards of silk.

The Nepalese maid clapped her hands with delight, then brought flowers from a table near the door to arrange them at the back of Chandra's hair.

Tonight she made no effort at a fashionable coiffure but instead parted her hair in the middle and let it wave as it did naturally on each side of her forehead and arranged it only in a high, thick chignon at the back of her head.

Her maid fixed the flowers on either side of the chignon, and when Chandra gazed at herself in the mirror she knew that she had never looked more attractive or more unusual.

In fact, she appeared so unlike herself that she felt shy of letting Lord Frome or anyone else see her.

"Is there a party tonight?" she asked the maid.

The Nepalese girl shook her head and Chandra felt relieved.

At the same time, in some ways it made it more difficult to go downstairs and meet Lord Frome's eyes.

Because time was getting on, she knew that she must not be late for dinner, and at last she made the effort.

Slowly she walked down the big staircase and crossed the hall, wondering if the servants in their red and white uniforms thought it strange that she should be in their native dress.

The door of the Reception-Room was open and she saw the two men standing at the far end of the room, with glasses in their hands.

Slowly she walked towards them, conscious as she did so that no-one could walk in a sari without being graceful. Although she wanted, because she was shy, to bend her head and drop her eyes, she walked with her head high and her chin up.

The Resident came to meet her.

"My dear Lady Frome!" he exclaimed. "May I congratulate you on your appearance! I have never seen an Englishwoman who looked so right or indeed so beautiful in a sari!"

Chandra smiled at his compliment; then, almost compelled against her will, she looked at Lord Frome.

For a moment it was difficult, in a way which she could not understand, to see his face.

Then she saw that he was smiling and there was undoubtedly an unexpected glint of admiration in his eyes.

Chapter Six

As they were reaching the end of the Temples and the houses where they could still ride side-by-side, Lord Frome broke the long silence and said to Chandra:

"I have bad news for you."

She looked at him in surprise and he explained:

"We have to leave tomorrow!"

"Tomorrow?" she ejaculated. "I cannot believe it! But why? What has happened?"

"The Prime Minister has refused to extend our permit."

"Why should he do that? He and his wife have been so charming to us. Only last night she suggested that we dine with them in a few days' time."

"I do not suppose the Prime Minister discusses affairs of Government with his wife," Lord Frome said drily.

"But why should he refuse to allow us to stay?" Chandra asked.

"I have been informed that it is Government policy, which of course is true," he answered. "But I was quite certain, in fact I was told, that it would be easy if we could persuade her to get the Prime Minister to allow us to stay as long as we wished."

"Then why should he change his mind?"

"There could be various reasons," Lord Frome replied, "but I think in fact he agrees with the Resident that the Sanskrit manuscripts should be kept in the Monasteries and not be allowed to leave the country."

Chandra gave a deep sigh.

"I suppose one can understand their point of view," she said. "At the same time, what good are they doing just lying on the shelves getting dusty, with the thoughts they contain not having a chance to reach the outside world?"

"Which would pay little attention to them anyway," Lord Frome said drily.

Chandra knew that this was true, but she felt with a sense of despair that it was tragic that their work should come to an end so quickly.

During the last few days it had been a delight beyond anything she could express to work in the Library at one of the Monasteries and discuss with Lord Frome the merits of every manuscript they examined.

Besides, there was always at the back of their minds the hope that at any moment they might find the Lotus Manuscript.

When they had returned to the Residency there was either a party being given for them by Colonel Wylie or they dined in one of the huge Palaces which belonged to the family of the Prime Minister.

Chandra, to her delight, had seen the leaping fountains that were illuminated with coloured lights, and had found that many of the treasures in the huge Palaces were centuries old and so beautiful that she longed for Lord Frome to take them back with him when they left the country.

Perhaps, she thought now, that was one of the things they were afraid he might do which had resulted in the Prime Minister curtailing his visit to Nepal.

The more she got to know the Nepalese, the more

she realised that they wished their country to be kept secret and closed to foreigners.

They were completely happy in their own small Eden and did not wish the encroachment of alien people with their revolutionary ideas.

At the same time, it was a shock to know that they must leave without having attained their main objective.

They had ridden for some minutes before Chandra said:

"That means there is only today to find what we seek."

"And there are still thousands of manuscripts we have not yet examined," Lord Frome said.

"Could you not see the Prime Minister yourself and plead with him to let us stay a little while longer?" Chandra suggested.

As she spoke, she knew that where she was concerned it would be almost an agony to leave this enchanted place and the work she was doing with Lord Frome.

When they were actually in the Monastery he seemed a different person from who he was outside.

Excited by the manuscripts they examined together, he would talk with an enthusiasm which was quite different from his somewhat grim reserve at other times.

Now, Chandra thought, they would only have that tough, difficult journey back over the mountains, and once they reached India, Lord Frome would say goodbye to her and she would never see him again.

The knowledge that this lay ahead gave her a strange feeling which she had never had before.

She did not wish to explain it even to herself, but she knew that she would remember this visit to Nepal all the days of her life, and although she was ashamed to admit it, the Manor House where she lived and where there was little to do but worry over money would seem, in contrast, drab and dull.

'I shall be with Papa,' she thought.

But she knew, although it was hard to face the truth, that when her father was well he was quite self-sufficient without her, while Lord Frome needed her.

Any doubts Lord Frome might have had about her ability had been swept away, and he deferred to her judgement over every manuscript they took from the shelves.

He had never questioned her authority because of her age, as another scholar of equal learning might have done.

"I shall miss him," she told herself.

She rode behind him when the road narrowed, and once again they met the peasants coming into town from the countryside.

To some of the peasants they were already a familiar sight, and they smiled and nodded as they hurried by at their jog-trot, which never varied and which Chandra knew they could keep up not only for hours but for days on end.

They reached the Monastery, and after the usual greeting of trumpets played by Monks, and the Lama waiting at the gateway, they were left alone in the Library.

Chandra pulled off her hat and jacket, for it was very warm, then stood looking round at the shelves.

"As this is our last chance," she said after a moment, "to find the Lotus Manuscript, you would think that one would feel its holiness vibrating towards us and that we should be drawn to it automatically."

"What do you feel?" Lord Frome asked unexpectedly.

She was surprised at his question, thinking that he might instead have laughed at her for being fanciful.

"I feel," she answered, "as if everything round us is good and has something to say, to which we should listen, but there is nothing that draws me particularly, nothing I feel that vibrates with an ... inescapable sanctity."

She gave a little sigh.

"It must be that I am not advanced enough spiritually for an awareness of the Lotus Manuscript."

There was silence before Lord Frome said:

"We will just pick out something at random. I have already agreed with the Abbot to buy all those we have chosen so far, and he is delighted at the sum he will receive."

"Do you think he knows that the Lotus Manuscript is in the Monastery?" Chandra asked in a low voice.

"I have no idea," Lord Frome answered, but I could not mention it to him."

"No, of course not," she agreed.

As she spoke she reached up to take a manuscript from the shelf.

It was wrapped in a lovely piece of embroidered Chinese silk, but the contents did not justify the wrapping, and after she had looked at it she put it back from where she had taken it.

Perhaps it was because she was over-eager, Chandra thought several hours later, that today they had been unlucky.

The manuscripts they examined were not particularly interesting and it was only after luncheon that Lord Frome found one that appeared to be of importance.

Chandra picked it up and began to translate it to herself.

She took so long that Lord Frome said impatiently: "Well? Is it worthwhile?"

"It is wonderful!" Chandra cried. "Quite wonderful!"

"Why?" he enquired.

"It is very old," she said after a moment, "and written almost like a poem, and it is called, unless I am mistaken: 'The Song of the Celestial Soul.' "

She was sitting at the table as she read it, and Lord Frome bent over her to say:

"You are certain that that is the right translation? It sounds different from anything else we have found."

"It is different," Chandra said, "and I know Papa would be thrilled to translate it for you. It is very old and is written in the difficult Sanskrit at which he excels."

"Then we must certainly take it back to him," Lord Frome said.

"He will be very excited," Chandra replied, "and it will at least be some compensation if we cannot find the Lotus Manuscript."

"We still have a little while left," Lord Frome said, looking at his watch, "so do not let us waste any more time."

Chandra wrapped up the manuscript at which they had been looking and left it in the centre of the table, then once again went towards the shelves.

As she did so, the door of the room opened and there entered a Lama whom they had never seen before but whom she recognised at once as a man of great importance.

He was tall, far taller than the Abbot of the Monastery, and robed and hooded in yellow, while the other Monks wore red. One shoulder was bare and from it the drapery fell to his feet.

He stood for a moment looking at them, then threw back his hood, and as Chandra saw his shaven head and his face, she knew that he was different from any of the other Monks and Lamas they had met already.

He gave the impression of power and also of such spiritual attainment that instinctively, without even thinking, she put her hands palm to palm and made the greeting of *Namaskar,* raising her fingers to her forehead.

"Greetings, my children!" the Lama said in a deep voice, and to Chandra's surprise he spoke English.

No-one else in the whole Monastery whom they had met so far had spoken anything but their own language.

He did not wait for their reply, but said to Chandra, as he looked at what lay on the table:

"I see you have found 'The Song of the Celestial Soul.' It is a work that you must take to your Honourable father, and it will bring him great merit both in this world and those to come."

Chandra knew that Lord Frome was extremely surprised and she could almost read his thoughts of how extraordinary it was that this Lama whom they had never seen before should talk as if he was familiar with them and with the Professor.

The Lama now addressed Lord Frome.

"I know you are disappointed, My Lord, that you must leave tomorrow," he said, "but as it happens, there is no more for you to do here."

"But we have not been able to look at half the manuscripts we would have liked to examine," Lord Frome replied.

"I know what you seek," the Lama said, "but all your searchings in this room will not find it."

Both Chandra and Lord Frome looked at him in a startled manner as he went on:

"But because. I believe your interest is not selfish, but for the good of mankind, I will show you what you wish to see, even though you may not take it with you."

"You are referring to the Lotus Manuscript?" Lord Frome asked in a carefully controlled voice.

"We have other names for it, more sacred ones," the Lama answered, "and I will not ask you how you knew it was here in this Monastery. I will inform you only that because such a closely guarded secret has reached your ears, I must take it elsewhere."

To Chandra's surprise, Lord Frome smiled.

"I did not really believe I should have the good fortune to be able to take it away unnoticed."

A faint smile curved the Lama's lips.

"That, My Lord, would have been impossible!" he said. "And it is not yet time for the world to learn of the contents of this sacred manuscript. One day men's minds will be big enough to hear and understand the truth it contains, but not now."

He looked at Chandra, saw the disappointment in her eyes, and said quietly:

"Be content, my child, with the good that will come from your father's translation of 'The Song of the Celestial Soul'; and so that you will not go unrewarded for the work you have done, come with me."

He made a gesture with his hand which included both of them, and they followed him through an open door and down several long, dark passages that were like rabbit-warrens.

There was no-one else to be seen, and Chandra felt that perhaps it was an order that they should move quietly, as if through time and space with no-one to watch them.

Then at last their guide, who had walked silently in front of them, turned to pass through an open door which led into a small Temple.

It was so small that Chandra felt it was like a Chapel, and she knew that it was the Temple that must be in the heart of the building and where the Abbot himself worshipped.

At first it was difficult to see anything but two or three flickering lights which were just wicks in bowls of oil.

Then she saw towering towards the ceiling a huge statue of Buddha.

He sat enthroned on a lotus, and as Chandra looked up at the serene face, she could feel, as she had not felt in the Library, great waves coming towards her which were magnetically inescapable.

Because it was very awe-inspiring and at the same time so exciting that she felt as if she could hardly breathe, she moved almost unconsciously a little closer to Lord Frome and slipped her hand into his.

She felt his fingers close over hers, and she knew as he touched her that he was as excited as she was.

In front of them the Lama knelt in prayer before the great figure of the Buddha, then he rose up to take something from the upturned hands.

The Lama turned round, holding a narrow wooden box carved with strange hieroglyphs.

There was no need for either Chandra or Lord Frome to ask what the box contained. It was obvious from the way the Lama held it and in the expression on his face.

They took a step forward to stand directly in front of him. Then slowly, reverently, he raised the lid of the box and they saw lying inside it, on a bed of satin, the manuscript that they had sought.

Chandra knew that it was written on palm-leaves and even at a glance she could tell how immensely old it was.

There was something else, something that emanated from it which was so vital, so vibrant, that she knew that if it had been in the Library they would have been drawn to it irresistibly from the first moment they had entered the room.

Instinctively, still holding on to Lord Frome's hand, Chandra went down on her knees, and with hardly a second's pause he knelt beside her.

"Now you have seen what you were seeking," the Lama said very quietly, "and have been privileged as few others have been, and certainly as no-one who is not of our faith has been. Remember it in your hearts, but keep what you have seen to yourselves, for there are always those who would spoil and destroy that which is too sacred for them to understand."

He bent down a little lower so that they could look for a long moment at the manuscript. Then he closed the box and set it back in the Buddha's hands, from which he had taken it.

When he had done so, the Lama stood still, with his back to them, looking up at the face of the Holy One, whose head almost touched the ceiling.

As Chandra and Lord Frome rose to their feet, she knew that the Lama had no wish to speak to them again.

She did not know how she knew, she just had a strong conviction within her that he had said all he had to say. He had given them the inestimable gift of seeing the sacred manuscript with their own eyes, and now it was time for them to go.

She drew Lord Frome by the hand, and as if he understood he made no protest, and in silence they walked back down the passages.

Chandra felt that they might have mistaken the way back, but suddenly the Library door was in front of them and they went in.

Only then did she take her hand from Lord Frome's, and she felt as if they had been linked together in some special ceremony from which they had emerged different in themselves, although it would be hard to explain in what way.

Without speaking, because she felt that the sound of a voice would jar on the feelings within her heart and her mind, Chandra picked up the manuscript they had left on the table and looked at Lord Frome questioningly.

He spoke for the first time.

"I will see the Abbot. Wait for me at the gate."

He left the Library and went down the passage which Chandra knew led to the part of the Monastery to which she could not be admitted.

She walked to the courtyard in which there was the main gate, where their ponies were waiting.

There was also a number of Monks, who smiled happily at the sight of her, their black eyes full of curiosity and interest.

She talked to them and they asked her questions about the land where she lived and many other things besides.

Whatever she replied, her answers made them laugh, and she thought that many of them were just young boys who found life a huge adventure even though they were confined to a Monastery where they did little but pray and perform the ordinary chores that were required in the great building.

She had not been with them long before Lord Frome appeared, accompanied not by the Abbot but by the Senior Lama who had greeted them on their arrival.

He said good-bye to Chandra with an old-world charm that she thought was worthy of a diplomat, and then to the roar of trumpets they started down the steep mountain path which led to the valley.

Once again they had to ride single-file on the raised road, and even when they reached Katmandu the streets were so crowded that it was impossible to have any conversation.

"We will talk about it when we get back to the Residency," Chandra told herself, and yet she wondered what she should say to Lord Frome.

It was difficult for her to sort out her own thoughts and feelings about what had occurred.

In a way it was very wonderful, and she knew that even though they could never handle or possess the Lotus Manuscript, to have seen it, to know that it really did exist, was a wonder almost beyond words.

They reached the Residency and learnt the moment they entered the front door that a huge good-bye party was being given for them that evening, and there would be only just time for them to bathe and change before they had to be downstairs in the Reception-Room.

Chandra hurried to her bedroom, wondering which of the lovely saris Lord Frome had given her she should wear this evening.

She had worn them all once, the pink, the green, and the blue, and it was difficult to know which was the most becoming, as they were all so attractive.

Then as her maid greeted her, she saw laid out for her on the bed another sari, and this, she thought, was more beautiful than any she had ever seen.

"Is this for me?" she cried, knowing the answer.

The Nepalese maid giggled, which meant she was happy.

"Present from Lord Sahib," she said. "Very special sari come today."

It was indeed very special, Chandra thought, for the sari was a golden yellow which reminded her of the sunshine and it was embroidered all over with pearls and tiny topazes, while the borders were deep with gold thread and larger topazes.

It was so lovely, and at the same time she thought that it must have been so expensive that she could not possibly accept anything so valuable.

Then she knew that whatever anyone might say, however reprehensible it might be, she could not refuse anything so beautiful.

She had her bath and put on the sari, and she knew that with her strange-coloured hair nothing could have been more attractive or more becoming.

Her maid had brought her some small yellow lilies which grew in profusion in the garden and which were exactly the same colour as the sari.

She arranged them as she had before, at the back of Chandra's head, and as she stood up to look at herself in the long mirror there was a knock on the communicating-door.

Never since the night she had gone to Lord Frome to apologise to him had the door been opened

Now as she said: "Come in!" she wondered, as she had wondered before, whether he was as conscious that she was so near as she was conscious of him.

He came into the room looking, she thought, even more magnificent than usual, for he was wearing a number of decorations which she had not seen before.

He sood looking at her and she said a little shyly:

"I . . . I do not know how to . . . thank you . . . I did not believe it was possible to find a sari more beautiful than those you have given me already . . . but this one is . . . unbelievable!"

"The man from whom I bought it," Lord Frome said, "told me he brought it especially from India to offer it to the Queen. It once belonged to a Rajput Princess and is in fact over a hundred yeard old! I thought that was why you would like it."

"I love it!" Chandra exclaimed. "And though I know I ought not to accept such a wonderful gift, it is something I . . . cannot refuse."

"I should be very hurt if you did," Lord Frome replied, "And I have bought you something to wear with it to commemorate the interesting time we have spent together and in particular what we experienced this afternoon."

She knew, as he spoke quietly and seriously, that she had been frightened, although she thought it unlikely, that he might laugh—perhaps mock the solemnity with which the Lama had handled the Lotus Manuscript.

She also thought he might be embarrassed by the strange feeling that they had both felt when they had knelt before the statue of Buddha.

But she knew now without being told that Lord Frome had been as moved as she had been.

Somehow she did not wish to discuss it at this moment, and as if he felt the same way, he opened the box he carried in his hand, and she saw that it contained a necklace of large graded topazes.

"It matches your dress," he said, as if that was an excuse for giving it to her.

"B-but . . . I cannot . . . I must not . . ." Chandra began.

Then with her eyes shining she said:

"It is lovely! I never thought . . . I never dreamt that I would own a necklace like this . . . oh . . . thank you . . . thank you!"

"It is part-payment for what I owe you," Lord Frome said, "because, as you realise by now only too well, I would not have found the manuscripts I have bought without you to guide me."

A sudden idea struck Chandra, and as she looked up at him he added, as if he read her thoughts:

"I have not forgotten your father and I have every intention of doing something for him. We will talk about it on our way home, but now we must not be late for dinner."

Chandra looked at him and her eyes expressed everything she could not say.

Then with a little cry of sheer delight she sat down on the stool in front of the dressing-table and put the necklace up to her neck.

"I will fasten it for you," Lord Frome said.

As she bent her head, he took the ends of the necklace from her hands and fastened it at the back of her neck.

And he did so, his fingers touched her skin and she felt a little quiver run through her.

It was something she had never felt before and she could not explain it, and when it had gone, she felt that she must have dreamed it.

"We must hurry," he said.

She rose to her feet, knowing that she had been looking at her own reflection in the mirror in a bemused fashion.

They walked across the room side-by-side, then as they went downstairs Chandra told herself that this might be the last time she would ever be at a party.

But if it was, she would always remember that she was confident that she would not be eclipsed by any other woman in the room, not even the Nepalese ladies adorned with their sparkling emeralds and rubies.

In fact, before the evening was out, she had been complimented hundreds of times on her sari.

The gentlemen told her that she looked like a goddess of the sun, and laughed when she replied that as her name was Chandra she was actually the goddess of the moon.

But the ladies when they were alone fingered the richly embroidered silk and exclaimed over the workmanship and the beauty of the topazes.

They stared with admiration at the stones in Chandra's necklace.

"Topazes are very lucky for those who can wear them," one lady told her, "and therefore, Lady Frome, you will always be lucky in love."

Chandra wanted to say that she had never known love and in fact had always been afraid that she would never find it.

But it was hardly something she could say when they thought Lord Frome was her husband, and several of them had already said how handsome he was and how charming to talk to.

When the time came to say good-bye, Chandra was very touched to find that all the Nepalese ladies had brought her presents.

There were little embroidered hand-bags, and a great number of the special Nepalese ornaments which were usually small birds with their wings set with coral and turquoises that were found in the mountains.

And there was also a strange stone which was characteristic of Katmandu, a smoky topaz, almost the colour, Chandra found, of her hair.

These they gave to her in small boxes, in brooches, and in rings. There was a pair of ear-rings, and one to match which she suspected was intended for her nose!

She would have been extremely embarrassed at having nothing to give in return when they were leaving, if Lord Frome had not produced a number of small flat envelopes.

Chandra could not think what they contained, until the ladies opened them and inside there were small silk handkerchiefs, each one embroidered at the corners with little bunches of flowers.

They were all delighted, and only when the last guest had left did Chandra say:

"How clever of you to have presents for them!"

"One should never travel in the East empty-handed," Lord Frome replied, "and I bought those handkerchiefs in India thinking I might require them."

"I was so thankful you had them," Chandra said, "but I had no idea that they would bring me such beautiful presents."

"You are one of the first English ladies to visit Nepal," Colonel Wylie said, "and certainly the most popular! I assure you that you will be talked about until you become almost a legend in Katmandu."

"I would have liked to ... stay a little ... longer," Chandra replied.

She saw the expression in the Resident's eyes and was quite certain that he had not used the weight of his authority to persuade the Prime Minister to extend their permit.

"There are a few things I would like to talk to you about, My Lord, before you retire," he said to Lord Frome.

Chandra, knowing that he did not wish her to be present, said good-night.

She felt sad that she must go, and yet she knew she had so much to remember, so much for which to be thankful.

She thought as she fell asleep that she had three days left with Lord Frome before everything would be finished.

There was a definite ache in her heart that was almost a physical pain before finally she drifted away into unconsciousness.

* * *

In the morning, having been called earlier than usual, Chandra had the greatest difficulty in dressing while she watched the sunshine striking the peaks of the Himalayas as they emerged above the encircling white clouds.

"Perhaps I shall never see them again," she told herself, and kept trying to put on her clothes without moving from the window.

Finally she was ready, and when she went downstairs she found that the Resident was having breakfast with them.

"I hope you will be able to return another year," he said to Lord Frome.

But Chandra was certain that he was merely being polite and that really he hoped nothing of the sort.

She noticed that he made no mention of the manuscripts which Lord Frome was carrying away with him, but she was certain that the Resident would not think they were leaving empty-handed and was resentful that his advice on the matter had not been taken.

It was only as she said good-bye not only to the Resident but also to his secretaries, his Aides-de-Camp, and his senior servants, shaking hands with them all, that Chandra suddenly remembered that she had never received the emerald that had been stolen by Nana Sahib.

She had actually forgotten about it in the last few days, in the excitement of searching amongst the manuscripts at the Monastery.

Now she wondered if whoever was supposed to hand over the gem realised that she was leaving sooner than might have been expected.

There was, however, nothing she could do about it.

She thanked those who had contributed so much to their pleasure, while she knew that Lord Frome was leaving a large amount of money to be distributed amongst the servants.

The ponies they had brought with them were all waiting outside the front door, the boxes strapped on their backs, their *syces* standing at their heads.

Chandra waited for someone to help her into the saddle, but before her own *syce* could do so, one of the Residency servants in his red and gold livery moved forward.

He helped her up, and then as she put out her hand to take the reins, she felt something pressed into her left hand.

Almost automatically her fingers closed over a hard object, and then as she looked for the face of the man who had given her what she had expected, he seemed to have disappeared into the crowd of people standing on the steps waiting to see them depart.

Lord Frome mounted and rode ahead and she followed behind him as they had done on their ride into Katmandu.

As they rode down the short drive which led to the gate, there was a cheer from the Residency steps and everybody's arms were raised in farewell.

Only when they were outside the Residency territory did Chandra look down to see what she held in her left hand.

It was a small chamois bag and she could feel that it contained something hard. She only cast a quick glance at it in case any of the *syces* following should notice what she was doing.

Then she undid two buttons on the front of her

blouse and slipped the bag through to let it lie against the bare skin between her breasts.

She thought it unlikely that anyone had seen her swift action.

Now they were amongst the crowds in the streets of Katmandu, and as Lord Frome moved swiftly ahead, Chandra forced herself not to think of what had come into her possession.

She concentrated on her last glimpse of the exquisitely painted pagoda Temples, the wooden houses with their elaborate carvings round the balconies and the windows, and gave one last good-bye to Kala Bhairab, looking fiercer and more frightening, she thought, than when she had last seen him on her arrival.

Then they were climbing away from the town and up towards the Churia Mountains in the distance.

They were covered with clouds and Chandra thought that it was somehow significant that while the mountains behind them were dazzling in the sunshine, those ahead were shrouded as if in sadness.

"Why must we go? Why must we go?" her pony's hoofs seemed to be saying, as if in echo to the words that were being expressed over and over in her heart.

Once again they found the rice-fields planted on the gigantic steps that had been cut up the side of the mountain.

They passed the tiny brown earth huts with their straw roofs, and all the way along the stony, rising road they met the men and women with their heavy loads on their backs, held by a forehead strap, hurrying either up or down the mountain.

They seemed to Chantra to move at the same pace whichever way they were going.

They all smiled and seemed very happy and Chandra noticed how many of them said a prayer at the small stone *Chaityas* which had been built every half-a-mile or so along the path over the mountain.

They stopped for a midday meal and Chandra, looking back over the valley, which was now a long way beneath them, said in a low voice to Lord Frome:

"As you anticipated, we have been thrown out of your Eden, not by an angel with a flaming sword but by the Prime Minister, who seemed such a very pleasant little man."

"We might have known from the very beginning that it was too good to last!" Lord Frome replied.

He spoke lightly, but she knew that he minded as she did that they could not have stayed any longer.

"Perhaps we should be grateful that we found so ... much," Chandra said, "and do not forget that the Lama with the Lotus Manuscript said that 'The Song of the Celestial Soul,' which you discovered, will do a great deal of good in the world."

"Do you really believe that?" Lord Frome asked. "The manuscripts that have been published so far have certainly not aroused the slightest interest except amongst scholars."

"There must always be a first time," Chandra replied, "and if he said it will happen ... it will!"

"I can see that you were impressed by him."

"No-one could fail to be," she answered. "I would love to know who he is."

"I have no idea," Lord Frome said, "but he was a Keeper of the Manuscripts and therefore I should imagine a man of great intelligence and perhaps one of those who, we are told, are sent back to this world to help those who must be left behind."

Chandra looked at him in sheer astonishment.

She knew he referred to the Masters who were so advanced in the spiritual world that they elected to return to earth to help those who sought the truth but needed a teacher.

She would never have imagined that there was anybody except her father with whom she could discuss such things.

Yet, because of her work on the Buddhist manuscripts, she believed that there were such Gurus, if only one could find them.

After a moment she asked:

"You have practised Yoga?"

Lord Frome nodded his head.

"When?"

She did not know why she was so eager to know.

"A long time ago," he replied. "Something happened in my life which started me on my search for manuscripts, and at the first Monastery I visited, which was in Tibet, I was allowed to stay with them for two years."

As he finished speaking he rose to his feet and called for the servants to pack up what remained of their luncheon.

As they rode on, Chandra found herself putting what he had told her into place in her mind as though she had found another piece of the puzzle which was Lord Frome.

It must have been, she told herself, after his heart had been broken that he had gone away, perhaps on a world tour, as men have done since the beginning of time, and found his way to Tibet.

He must have been guided there, and the Yoga he had practised would have helped him to forget and aroused instead an insatiable desire to study precious manuscripts which in many Monasteries were neglected or forgotten.

She had never before suspected that there had been any ulterior reason behind Lord Frome's travels except that he collected manuscripts as other rich men collected pictures or objets d'art.

Now it struck her that he had another, very vital reason—the desire to help those who were still deaf to the great truths which were known to many in the East, but to which the West had sadly turned a deaf ear.

'I want to talk to him, and I want to know a great deal more,' Chandra thought to herself.

Then she felt despairingly that she might not get the opportunity even though they would be alone at dinner in the primitive Dak-Bungalow where they had stayed before.

They had climbed higher and now they were entirely encircled by the clouds.

Moving through the soft, moist air gave Chandra a strange feeling, as if she were in a dream.

She could only just see Lord Frome ahead, and the trail of ponies behind were out of sight, and yet when they reached the Dak-Bungalow where they had stayed before, it looked just as squalid and dirty and the children who ran up and greeted them were in the same tattered rags.

Chandra herself, however, felt different from the way she had before. Then she had been utterly and completely exhausted by the ride; now she was barely tired at all.

Also, having ridden to the Monastery every day, she was no longer stiff from being so many hours in the saddle.

She went to the room where she had slept before, to change, and she saw that the keeper of the Bungalow had not even brushed the floor since she had last used it.

But she was not really interested in anything except that she had been conscious all afternoon of what lay between her breasts.

She pulled off her hat and jacket, and then before she undressed any further she drew out the bag and opened it.

She sat down on the bed on which Mehan Lall had arranged her quilt and blanket and tipped what the bag contained onto the pillow.

Then she gave a little gasp. It was as if something alive lay against the white linen.

Never had she seen a larger emerald or one with such depth.

It was oval in shape, to represent the third eye in the Buddha's forehead, and without being in the least knowledgeable about gems, she knew that because it was unflawed, it was a unique stone in its brilliance.

It was not surprising that Nana Sahib, being a connoisseur of jewels, had wanted to possess it.

Chandra looked at the emerald for a long time, then put it back in the small bag, knowing that she carried a great fortune, if one could value anything so sacred in terms of money, and not for one second must it leave her possession.

She took it with her when she went to the sluice to wash away the dust from the journey.

When she went back to her bedroom to put on the plain gown she had worn the first night she had dined with Lord Frome, she placed it once again between her breasts.

She would have liked to wear one of her beautiful saris, if only because it was the last time Lord Frome would see them.

But she had packed them very carefully in her trunk and she would not have them creased in the bag in which she carried the things she needed just for the two nights on the road.

She did, however, hesitate for a moment as to whether she would add her topaz necklace to the dress with its demure, Puritan collar.

Then she thought that it would look out-of-place and ridiculous, and Lord Frome would not understand that she was still trying to thank him for giving her anything so lovely.

Therefore, she went into dinner looking very different from the way she had the night before, but she told herself that it was unlikely Lord Frome would notice her one way or another.

It was just being conceited even to think that he might.

As she entered the small Dining-Room he said:

"I have a better choice of drinks for you tonight. There is a little wine which I thought we might drink at dinner, and I also have some Nepalese brandy which is not unlike a good sherry. I think you would like that as an appetiser."

She accepted the glass from him and found that the brandy was quite pleasant.

Then dinner was ready, and it was almost identical to what they had eaten at the first Dak-Bungalow at which they had stayed.

"I knew it would be hot soup and chicken!" Chandra exclaimed, and they both laughed as if at some private joke.

They talked about Nepalese customs during the dinner and Chandra found that what Lord Frome told her about them was so interesting that she wished she had thought to question him when they were in Katmandu.

'We wasted so much time fighting,' she thought to herself, 'when I should have been pleading with him to tell me about the country and its people.'

She could not put back the clock, but she plied Lord Frome with questions and was thrilled by some of the legends which now seemed so very real because she had seen the people of Nepal and the way they lived.

She felt that she could understand how so many of their beliefs had arisen in that happy valley.

When they had finished dinner she was sure that Lord Frome was conscious of the time, and, knowing what was expected of her, she said:

"I think, as we will be leaving early, My Lord, I should retire."

"We must certainly try to get some sleep tonight," he answered, "for it will be a long day tomorrow. As you know, we have to pass quickly through the valley, where it is dangerous to linger because of the risk of catching malaria."

"I was told that when we came through it before, and rather than have malaria I am prepared to gallop all the way."

Lord Frome smiled.

"I doubt if your pony will let you do that," he replied. "But we will certainly start early, and I hope you do not get too tired this time."

There was a considerate note in his voice, which made her feel shy.

She said good-night and went to her room.

It was cold enough for her to appreciate the quilt, which she folded in two. She lay on one half of it and covered herself with the other.

She also was glad to have the blanket over her as well.

When she had taken off her dress, she hesitated as to what to do with the emerald; then, finding a long piece of ribbon amongst her things, she hung the bag from it and tied the ribbon round her neck.

'It will be safe there,' she thought, slipping it under her lawn nightgown.

In bed, Chandra shut her eyes and started to think of the interesting things Lord Frome had told her at dinner.

It was not only what he had said, she thought, it was because he sounded so attractive when he spoke in his deep voice, which now, because they had become friends, was no longer harsh and hard as it had been when they had first met.

'I could learn so . . . much from him!' she thought drowsily, and fell asleep . . .

* * *

Chandra awoke feeling as if someone had spoken to her, then realised that everything was very quiet.

There was no sound in her small room, nor was there any sound from outside where her window looked out onto the courtyard.

And yet she was awake—wide awake!

Then quite clearly, although she knew he was not speaking except in her mind, she heard the Lama Teshu.

"There is danger, my daughter!" he said to her. "Danger! Rise and go to the Lord Sahib!"

It was as real as if he were actually in the room, speaking to her, and Chandra felt that she could almost see him—his eyes looking into hers as they had done when she had sat at his feet and he had told her what was required of her.

"Danger!" the Lama repeated. "Do as I tell you! Go at once to the Lord Sahib!"

It was a command which Chandra knew she must obey.

Without thinking, without stopping to consider what she was doing, she got out of bed and moved in the darkness towards the door.

She had heard the sounds of Lord Frome going to bed because there was only a thin wooden partition between their bedrooms.

She stepped into the passage, which was in darkness, and felt her way to the next door.

She opened it, and only as she stepped inside the room did she wonder vaguely, far away at the back of her mind, what Lord Frome would think and if he would understand.

"Who is there?"

She heard Lord Frome's voice and for a moment found it difficult to answer him, but then she replied:

"It is I . . . Chandra."

"Chandra? What is the matter?"

He sat up in bed, and she heard him groping on the table beside him for a match with which to light the candle.

The light seemed to flood over the small room, and Lord Frome, leaning on his elbow, saw Chandra standing just inside the open door, her eyes wide in her pale face, her hair falling over her white night-gown.

"What has upset you?" he asked.

"There is . . . danger," she said. "I know . . . there is danger . . . and I am afraid!"

Lord Frome did not ask any questions. He quickly got out of bed, picked up his robe which lay on the end of his quilt, and put it on.

Then he took something from beside the candle, and Chandra saw that it was a pistol.

She did not say anything, but merely moved to one side as, lighting up the candle in his left hand, he passed her and went out into the passage.

She was still left with enough light to see that the only chair in the room was covered with his clothes, and she moved in her bare feet towards the bed and sat down on the end of it.

As she did so, she thought she had made a fool of herself, for there would be no-one in her room, no sign of any intruder.

Lord Frome would think she was an hysterical woman and would despise her for it.

She could not bear to arouse again the contempt he had once felt for her, and yet she told herself that it had been impossible to disobey the Lama.

She had known that he was speaking to her, known that she was in danger because of what she carried against her breast.

As she thought of it, she put her hand over the little bag, somehow feeling that it could help her and per-haps make Lord Frome understand that she was not just being foolish and imaginative.

He seemed to be away a long time. She knew he was still in her room, for there was still just a flicker of light from the candle he carried.

How could it take him so long, she wondered, to find that there was nothing unusual in the room she had just left?

And yet the Lama had told her that there was danger, and the Lama would not have been mistaken.

Chandra wondered frantically what she would do if Lord Frome said she had to return to her room, and she had no viable excuse for not doing so.

Then she heard his footsteps returning and the light came nearer as he moved down the passageway.

As he came into the bedroom, Chandra tried to see by the expression on his face what he was thinking.

Because she was nervous and afraid, she rose to her feet, feeling like a school-girl about to be reprimanded for making an unnecessary scene.

Lord Frome put first the candle and then the pistol back on the table beside the bed, then he turned round.

He had his back to the light, and as Chandra lifted her face to his in a desperate effort to see the expression in his eyes, he stood for a moment, looking at her.

Then, as she wanted to speak, wanted to ask him if he had found anything, he put out his arms and pulled her roughly against him.

She was so surprised, so astonished, that she felt as if in that one movement he took all the breath from her body.

Then before she could even murmur, his lips came down on hers and held her captive.

Chapter Seven

For a moment his lips so hurt Chandra that she was conscious that his kiss was almost a pain.

Then suddenly she felt a wild rapture that was inexpressible rising up through her body from her breasts to her lips.

She knew then, although she had not realised it, that this was what she had wanted, what she had longed for, and it was somehow linked with the wonder of the Lotus Manuscript and the beauty of Nepal.

His lips grew softer and yet more insistent, more demanding, and she felt, as he held her closer and still closer in his arms, that he drew her very heart from between her lips and made it his.

'This is love,' she thought, 'love as I always knew it would be if I could ever find it.'

At last, after what might have been a century of time, Lord Frome raised his head.

"My darling!" he exclaimed in a voice which she did not recognise. "I might have lost you!"

She looked up at him enquiringly, so bemused and bewildered by what had occurred that it was difficult to think.

Then he said:

"When I went into your room there was a *Khukri* struck in the centre of the bed. It must have been meant for me."

It took Chandra a moment to realise what he was talking about. Then she exclaimed:

"No . . . no! It was for . . . me! I must . . . tell you . . . why."

Even as she spoke, she thought of the wide-bladed, curved knives which the Nepalese men wore at their waists, and she knew that the Lama had been right in telling her that there was danger.

She shivered and Lord Frome said:

"You are cold, my precious. Get into bed, then we will talk."

His arms loosened as he spoke. At the same time, as if he could not bear to let her go, he moved his lips against her forehead and she felt herself quiver with a strange sensation she had never known before.

She was too ecstatic at the moment to feel cold, and yet she knew that, high as they were in the clouds, it was bitterly cold outside the Bungalow.

She sat down on the bed, then found that Lord Frome's quilt was different from her own. His was made in such a way that it was possible to slip right inside it, so that it was like a large sleeping-bag.

Because she wanted to obey him and also she was afraid that he might send her back to her own room, she got inside the thickly quilted, warm cover, and as she did so he went to the door.

He locked it and placed against it the chair on which were his clothes. Then he came back and looked at her in the candlelight.

"You . . . will be . . . cold," she said a little incoherently, conscious that the expression on his face made her feel shy and yet at the same time wildly excited.

He smiled.

"Fortunately, I travel ready for every emergency," he replied, "even for such as this."

He went to a corner of the bedroom where some of

his luggage was piled and drew from the top of a case another quilt like the one which covered Chandra, and also a thick woollen blanket.

He brought them back to the bed, and, having wrapped the quilt round him, he lay beside Chandra and covered them both with the blanket.

He put his arm round her shoulders and pulled her close to him.

"Now we can talk," he said, "and at the same time not catch pneumonia!"

There was something so gentle and considerate in his tone that Chandra felt she wanted to reach out her arms towards him and tell him how much she loved him.

But because she still felt shy, she put her head against his shoulder and tried to believe that this was really happening and was not part of a dream.

As if he understood what she was thinking, Lord Frome said very quietly:

"I love you! I have loved you for a long time, Chandra! But I have been fighting frantically against admitting it . . . even to myself."

"Do you . . . really love me?"

"I love you as I never thought I would ever love anybody," he answered, "and when just now I saw that *Khukri* in the centre of your bed, I knew that you meant everything in the world to me and I could no longer go on pretending to myself that I could live without you."

Chandra made a little sound of happiness, then she asked:

"When . . . did you fall in . . . love with me?"

Lord Frome's arms drew her a little closer as he said:

"I know now that it was when I picked you up off the floor in this very Bungalow and knew how brave and valiant you had been in riding for two exhausting days without complaining, without even asking me to go slower."

"I was so . . . ashamed that I . . . collapsed at the end," Chandra murmured.

"I was a brute to ask so much of you," Lord Frome replied. "It is something I will never do again."

As if he wanted to apologise but not in words, he put his hand under her chin and turned her face up to his.

"I love you!" he said. "And I will take much better care of you, my darling, than I have done so far."

His lips were on hers and she felt again that wonderful ecstasy that was so intense that it was half a pain and half a rapture.

Then, as his lips became more demanding, more possessive, she felt as if she wished to be closer to him, to become a part of him, even though she did not understand what she wanted.

Lord Frome took his lips from hers and said in a voice that was unsteady:

"I want you to explain to me, my sweet, why you think the *Khukri* was meant for you and not for me."

"I . . . I suppose it is something I should have . . . told you before," Chandra replied, "and perhaps you will be . . . angry with me for not . . . having done so."

"I will never be angry with you again," Lord Frome promised. "But you must forgive me for the way I behaved when you first told me you had come in your father's place."

"I knew you did not want me," Chandra said, "so I could understand how when I . . . turned up, it made you . . . cross."

"I have hated women for so long that I did not know how different you were, how very, very different, my precious one."

He kissed her again before he said:

"But we must try to keep to the point. Tell me why somebody—and I cannot really believe there is such a person—would wish to kill you."

In a very low voice, hesitating because she thought Lord Frome would not understand why she had done it, Chandra told him about the Lama Teshu and the Sakya-Cho Monastery, and how when they were actually leaving the Residency the emerald had been put into her hand.

He did not speak while she related all that had happened, and only when she finished speaking did his arm tighten round her, and he said:

"How could you take such risks with yourself when you belong to me?"

"I did not . . . know then that you would . . . love me," Chandra said with a little smile, "and I never thought, because I . . . hated you, that I would . . . love you."

"You do really love me now—you are sure of it?" Lord Frome enquired.

"I did not . . . know that love could be so . . . wonderful . . . so perfect!" she said. "Or that your kiss could make me feel as if you carried me up to the very peaks of the Himalayas."

"My precious darling!"

The words seemed to break from his lips.

Then he was kissing her again with slow, demanding kisses which became, as he felt her response, fierce and possessive.

Only when they were both breathless did he say:

"I will protect you so that we will take the emerald in safety to those to whom it belongs. At the same time, I will not let you have it any longer in your possession. You must give it to me."

Chandra hesitated.

"But . . . suppose," she asked, "suppose those who . . . want to steal it . . . strike again?"

"Then it would be better for me than for you to die," Lord Frome replied.

Chandra gave a little cry.

"Do you think I would let you do that?" she asked. "You are so . . . important in the world . . . and so is the work you do."

She knew he was about to protest, and she went on quickly:

"Besides, the Lama said I shall be protected, as I was just now when he told me, although you may not believe it, that I was to come to you."

"I do believe it," Lord Frome said, "and because you obeyed him, my darling heart, it saved your life."

Chandra smiled from sheer happiness because he believed that she had indeed been protected and did not try to put it down to her imagination as another man might have done.

"I want you to look after me," she said softly, "but I will keep the emerald round my neck because I know that if there is any danger for . . . me again, the Lama will warn me of it. Perhaps it would be more difficult for him to do so if I do not have the emerald in my . . . possession."

Lord Frome did not argue, but merely said:

"The emerald is precious to the Sakya-Cho Monastery, but you are far more precious to me. Therefore, I will protect you both, and although I am not clairvoyant, I believe we shall arrive safely at Bairagnia, and after that there will be no reason for thieves and robbers to pursue us."

"I shall always feel . . . safe with you," Chandra said.

"Which is what you will be," Lord Frome said, "but, darling, tonight and tomorrow night you must sleep beside me as you are now, for I will never again allow you to be in a room by yourself where you might be attacked."

"I . . . I would like . . . that," Chandra replied, "but it might be . . . uncomfortable for you."

"It may be uncomfortable," Lord Frome said, "and not only for the reason that the bed is very small. But we will be married at the first British Church we find in India, and then we can be together by night and day, my lovely one, without any more difficulties."

Chandra did not speak for a moment, but in the

light of the candle he could see her eyes shining with a radiance which seemed to transform her face.

Then she said a little hesitatingly:

"You are sure . . . quite sure that you . . . ought to . . . marry me?"

"I am quite sure that I intend to marry you."

"B-but you are a . . . woman-hater! You swore never to . . . m-marry."

He gave a little laugh and there was something almost boyish in it.

"I was so determined that I would never do so," he said, "that I might have known that sooner or later fate would deliberately send you to refute all such assertions."

Chandra turned her face against his shoulder.

"Papa told me that you had a . . . broken heart," she said, "and I wondered why nobody had ever been able to . . . repair it."

"Looking back, I do not think it was actually broken," Lord Frome said, "only slightly dented! What was really damaged was my pride and what you would call my self-conceit."

"What . . . happened?" Chandra asked.

"It is a banal story and I hardly like to repeat it," Lord Frome replied. "It is just that I thought I was in love with a girl to whom, because I was a young, idealistic fool, I wrote poems in the Byronistic vein and letters that were immaturely passionate."

There was the dry, mocking note in his voice that she had heard so often before, and Chandra asked:

"What . . . happened?"

"I discovered that the girl I was so busy idolising found my letters and my poems amusing enough to read aloud to her friends. What was more, she was secretly engaged to somebody else, although she did not trouble to acquaint me with the fact."

"That must have been very . . . hurtful."

"I was young enough to think it was a sword-thrust to my heart!"

"So you went round the world. That is what I . . .
thought you must have . . . done."

"It was the most sensible thing I ever did," Lord
Frome said. "It was in India that I first became interested in the Sanskrit manuscripts which inevitably took
me to Tibet."

"So out of evil came good!"

"I would hardly give it such a grand-sounding word
as 'evil,' " Lord Frome said, "but the young are very
vulnerable, which is exactly what I was."

"In a way . . . I am glad."

She thought there was an expression of surprise in
his eyes, and she explained:

"If you had married the girl to whom you wrote the
poems, you would be an old married man by now,
with perhaps a large number of children."

Lord Frome laughed.

"You are quite right, my darling!"

"And the Sanskrit manuscripts would still be forgotten in their Libraries," Chandra went on. "And so
much that is of importance would never have been
revealed to the world."

"What you are saying," Lord Frome said, "is that
'God moves in a mysterious way,' and I accept your
reasoning simply because I am so glad, so very, very
glad, my lovely one, that fate kept me for you."

"I . . . too am . . . glad," Chandra said, "except that
I cannot believe I shall not wake up to find that this is
all a dream and you are still . . . hating me because
you are . . . convinced that as a woman, I will not be
able to . . . help you in your . . . work."

Lord Frome drew her a little closer.

"We are going to work together always," he said,
"not only at the Sanskrit manuscripts but at something
far more important to us both."

"What is that?"

"Making a home for ourselves and perhaps 'the
large number of children' which I should have had if
I had been married when I was twenty-one!"

"I am . . . jealous when I . . . think of it," Chandra whispered.

"You need never be jealous of anyone," Lord Frome said firmly. "I have avoided all women for a very long time, and now, my darling . . . I am prepared to concentrate on you and you alone."

His lips were against her forehead as he spoke, then he kissed her eyes.

"You are so beautiful!" he said. "It is impossible for me even to look at another woman when you are in the room."

"I . . . I felt I looked . . . beautiful when I wore those lovely saris you . . . gave me," Chandra said, "but otherwise I know I am very nondescript compared to the . . . lovely ladies you must have met in England and in other countries."

Lord Frome kissed one of her cheeks before he said:

"You forget that I am used to looking for something different and unique in manuscripts, and therefore I have always found the so-called pretty or beautiful women of Society ordinary and somehow uninspiring."

He kissed her other cheek and went on:

"You inspire me in a way which I cannot explain. You also have a unique beauty that arouses me spiritually as well as physically."

Chandra gave a little exclamation.

"How could you say such . . . wonderful things to me?" she asked. "It is what I have wanted the man I loved to feel . . . but I never . . . never dreamt there would ever be one in the whole world who would . . . think like you."

"We were made for each other," Lord Frome said positively. "You are the other half of me, the part which has always been missing, which is why, my precious one, you have a lot of translating to do to make me as I ought to be."

"It will be . . . very exciting . . . work!"

He kissed each corner of her mouth, and then her lips, before he said:

"We have a great deal to discover about each other and it is going to take a lifetime before we know everything."

Every time Lord Frome kissed her, Chandra felt the sensations he aroused in her running through her like shafts of sunlight.

Once again she thought that she was like the peaks of the Himalayas with the sun turning them in the morning from white to pink and from pink to gold.

"You were ... telling me about the ... home we will make ... together," she said.

"I have a house which has been shut up for many years while I have been travelling," Lord Frome replied. "It is very old and I think very beautiful, but what it needs is a mistress; someone to care for it, someone who will bring it an atmosphere of happiness, which it has always lacked."

"Can ... I do that?" Chandra asked.

"We will do it together," he answered. "Now that I have found you, I know that happiness is based on two people—not one."

"You are quite ... quite sure that I can make you ... happy? It is very difficult for me to ... believe that I am really ... necessary to you."

"I will convince you how very necessary you are," he said. "But now, my precious one, I think you should try to go to sleep. We have a very long day in front of us tomorrow, and if I make you collapse for a second time, I would never forgive myself!"

"I feel as if I shall never be tired again," Chandra answered. "You have given my heart wings with which to fly through that frightening valley where there is malaria."

She paused, and then very shyly, in a voice he could hardly hear, she said:

"I shall want to ... ride very quickly ... so that

when we . . . arrive in the next Bungalow, I can be
. . . close beside you again . . . like this."

She knew that her words excited him.

Then he was kissing her again, kissing her until she
felt as though they were no longer in the small confined space but high in the sky, enveloped with the
light of love. . . .

*   *   *

It was a very long day's journey when Lord Frome
and Chandra rode through the valley where malaria
was prevalent to the Síságarhi Hill.

From the moment they left the clouds in the Churia
Mountains behind, Chandra felt herself protected and
knew that she need not really have any fears of either
of them being attacked.

Now, although she rode directly behind Lord Frome
as she had done before, Mehan Lall and his personal
servant walked on either side of her pony.

She knew that Lord Frome carried his pistol,
loaded, in his pocket, and there was a knife at Mehan
Lall's waist that had not been there before.

Now there was no question of Lord Frome hurrying
ahead of the rest of the baggage-train and she knew
that all the *syces* had been alerted to look out for any
enemy who might appear unexpectedly.

When they reached the Dak-Bungalow at Síságarhi
Hill, the *charpoy* from Chandra's bedroom was moved
into Lord Frome's and their beds were arranged so
close together that they could touch each other.

It was difficult for Chandra even now to realise how
deeply in love she was and how much Lord Frome
loved her.

And yet she had only to see the expression in his
eyes to feel her heart turn over in her breast.

When he touched her, she felt as if the shaft of
sunlight that was there every time he kissed her made
her whole body vibrate with new emotions she had
never thought it was possible to feel.

They talked together when they ate luncheon, and though it was a very quick meal she felt as if they ate ambrosia and drank nectar, and the world in which they sat near each other was a golden, dream-like place of unbelievable beauty.

Because she was in love, Chandra found that every flower, every tree, and every butterfly seemed different from how it had looked before.

They seemed to lift her mind to heights of inspiration that were inexpressible, and yet she knew she would be able to tell them to Lord Frome.

'I love you! I love you!' she thought as she looked at him riding ahead of her.

As if her love reached out and he felt it, he turned his head to smile at her and she knew that they were as close as if she were in his arms.

Only when at last the long day was ended and she could slip into the quilt on her bed and wait for him to come from the sluice where he was washing, did she think of how her whole world had changed and altered since she had gone to Nepal.

If her father had not been ill she would have been left at home with Ellen, seeing very few people, counting every penny they spent because the money which Lord Frome had given the Professor must last for a very long time.

Instead, a door into the world had suddenly opened before her.

She had found herself not only in one of the most fascinating countries she had ever imagined, but she had also had the privilege and glory of seeing the Lotus Manuscript and, more important than anything else, of finding love.

'It must all have been planned for me since the beginning of time,' she thought, and waited with her eyes on the door for Lord Frome to return.

He was taking such care of her that he had in fact locked her in before she had been left alone to undress and get into bed.

Before that, Mehan Lall had boarded up the window in the room so that it was impossible for anyone to enter in that way.

But, even having taken these precautions, Lord Frome had not left her unprotected, for his pistol lay beside her on the bed and he had instructed her in its use.

Because he was so loving and at the same time so understanding, Chandra thought that she had never had one moment of embarrassment when she was sleeping beside him.

She knew it was the only sensible thing to do, and she knew too that while he kissed her passionately and demandingly, he still treated her with a reverence that made her feel at times as if she were one of the fragile manuscripts they both handled so delicately.

"He loves me! He really loves me!" she told herself.

Although in many ways Chandra was very innocent, she knew that if Lord Frome had not been exactly the type of man he was, it would have been impossible for her to sleep beside him and not be afraid.

Now she heard him coming down the passage, and when, having turned the key in the lock of the door, he came into the room, her eyes were shining in the candlelight.

As he looked at her, he asked:

"How is it possible that you can be more lovely every time I see you? Each time I think that no woman could be more beautiful, and yet now when I look at you I know that you are much, much lovelier than you were a few minutes ago!"

Chandra smiled with sheer happiness.

But she knew with some intelligent part of her mind that when Lord Frome had forced upon himself a reserve and a hatred of all women, it had been like a fortified wall inside which he had enclosed himself.

Now the wall had fallen and everything that was poetic and idealistic in his nature had come to the surface, and he expressed himself in words that at times seemed like "The Song of the Celestial Soul," which they carried in their baggage.

She was sure that Lord Frome spoke to her not only with his heart but with his soul, and she wanted to give him in return everything she possessed: her mind, her heart, her soul, and . . . her body.

He walked across the room now to sit down on the side of her bed and say:

"I have been counting how many hours there are before we can be married."

"There is still . . . time for you to . . . change your mind," Chandra teased.

"Do you think that is possible?" he enquired. "You know as well as I do that I cannot escape not only from you, my darling, but also from fate."

"Do you . . . want to?"

"If I say more flattering things you will grow conceited," he answered, "and one of the things I love about you is that when anybody pays you a compliment, you blush."

As he spoke, he bent forward to find her lips, and although it was meant to be a light kiss, from the moment he touched Chandra they both felt the magnetic force that was inescapable drawing them closer.

Their need for each other was so strong, so irresistible, that it was almost violent in its intensity.

Lord Frome put his arms round Chandra and kissed her until she felt it was impossible to think.

She could only feel his love sweep over her like the waves of the sea, and she was drowning in an ecstasy that carried her down into the very depths of the ocean.

"I love . . . you! I love . . . you!"

She felt as though her whole body was crying the words, and when at length Lord Frome raised his head, with a fire in his eyes and his heart beating tumultuously, she looked up at him and felt as if the love that they had for each other blinded her.

"I must let you sleep," he said, as if he spoke to himself. "Oh, my darling, I want you! I need you! Thank God we have not to wait very much longer!"

He kissed her again, but gently, and then got into his own bed beside hers and turned to look at her for a long moment before he blew out the candle.

"I am ... praying that I shall always make you as ... happy as you are ... now," Chandra whispered.

"And I am praying that I will make you very much happier once you are my wife," he answered; "as happy as I shall be, because you are mine, completely and absolutely mine, and nobody shall ever take you from me!"

*   *   *

Chandra and Lord Frome arrived in Bairagnia a little earlier than they had expected because the route was downhill and, as Chandra remembered, much easier than at any other part of the road to Katmandu.

The flowers were even more beautiful, the orchids more profuse, and the trees gave them shade from the sun which had been lacking yesterday.

She knew that Lord Frome was a little apprehensive that the thick rhododendrons and other bushes might afford a hiding-place for robbers.

Mehan Lall and the other Indian servant walking beside her pony were also alert, their eyes searching for any movement amongst the trees or from behind protruding rocks.

They reached Bairagnia, however, without there being an incident of any sort, and Chandra felt that the Dak-Bungalow, which was so superior to the other two in which they had slept on Nepalese ground, was almost a Palace of luxury.

Now she was back in the India she loved, and she knew that if she could have chosen any place in the world in which to be married it would be there.

The luggage was taken into the same bedroom she had used on her outward journey, but Mehan Lall immdiately moved the *charpoy* into the next room, and then was intent on barring the window through which she had heard the little boy asking her to speak to the Lama.

This evening there would be no reason for anybody to call her, and she had already planned in her mind that as soon as they had finished their meal, she and Lord Frome would go together to find the Lama Teshu.

She was sure he would be waiting for her under the tree where he had been before.

But Lord Frome had already said that she was not to move outside the Bungalow or go anywhere unless he was with her.

The previous night Mehan Lall had slept outside their door, and when Chandra had protested that he would be uncomfortable, Lord Frome had merely replied:

"A good servant is always prepared to protect his master. When I showed Mehan Lall the *Khukri* which I found stuck in your bed, he himself offered to sleep outside our door."

Now while Chandra changed, Mehan Lall waited in the passage outside, so that she only had to call out should anything disturb her.

Perhaps such elaborate precautions were unnecessary. At the same time, it was comforting to know that those who might want to rob the Monastery of the sacred emerald would find it impossible to do so.

The dinner was ready and Chandra thought, as they ate the usual hot soup, chicken, and caramel pudding, that no French Chef could have provided a more delicious meal.

She knew it was because Lord Frome's eyes were looking into hers, and though they talked of ordinary things while the servants were in the room, their hearts were saying secret things to each other which nobody else would have been able to understand.

Lord Frome finished his glass of whisky, then said:

"Now, my darling, let us go and see if we can find the Lama who will relieve you of that dangerous jewel. I shall not have a moment's peace as long as I know you have it in your possession."

"I have been quite safe from the moment . . . you knew about it," Chandra answered.

"I am taking no chances where you are concerned," Lord Frome said determinedly, "and I have already told Mehan Lall and the other man that they are to come with us to the tree where your friend will be waiting."

"I shall feel rather uncomfortable arriving with an armed body-guard," Chandra said with a smile.

"I have told you I will take no risks," Lord Frome said, "and although I am prepared to argue with you, my precious, on a great number of subjects, I will not listen to anything which might constitute your being in any danger."

Because he spoke with such love in his voice, Chandra moved towards him and put her arms round his neck.

"How could I have imagined when I came into this room after I arrived, frightened of you and . . . terrified that you would send me home, that you would ever speak to me like . . . that?"

His arms went round her to pull her closely against him.

"It was what I wanted to do," he said, "but thank God I was afraid of losing my permit to visit Nepal."

He kissed her, then said:

"Come along, let us get this over. Then I shall try to believe that nobody is interested in you except myself."

She put her hand in his and he raised it to his lips.

"I also hope that in the future you will be interested in nobody except me," he added. "I find I am unbelievably jealous of an emerald, so Heaven knows what I should feel about any man who even looks at you!"

Chandra gave a little laugh. Then she said in a low voice:

"If there are any other . . . men in the world besides you . . . it would be impossible for me . . . to see them."

She knew by the expression on his face that Lord Frome was pleased by what she had said. Then as if he forced himself not to kiss her again, he pulled her by the hand out onto the verandah.

Two Indian servants who were waiting for them walked a few paces behind as Chandra and Lord Frome moved through the bushes towards the trees which stood on the edge of the Bungalow-garden.

As soon as she could see clearly through the shrubs, Chandra saw that she had not been mistaken in thinking that the Lama would be waiting for them.

He was there, sitting as he had been before, his back upright, his fingers touching the wooden rosary which hung from his waist.

Chandra and Lord Frome reached him, and as she stood in front of him, she put her arms together and raised her fingers to her forehead.

"Greetings, my daughter," the Lama said, "and to you, my son. The prayers of those in the Sakya-Cho Monastery have been answered, and our treasure has returned to us."

"I have it here for you," Chandra said, pulling over her head the ribbon to which the little chamois bag was attached.

She held it out to the Lama, who took it from her, and it disappeared immediately into the folds of his heavy, blanket-like robe. Then he said:

"I told you that you would be protected and that the merits you acquired in bringing back the jewel would also bring you the happiness you sought. That, I see, has come true."

"It has indeed!" Chandra answered, looking at Lord Frome.

The Lama nodded his head as if he had known about it already. Then he said:

"Your Honourable father will also be happy when he translates 'The Song of the Celestial Soul.' "

"How did you know we found that?" Chandra asked.

"These things are known," the Lama replied, "and so that he shall be free from the worries of the material world, I have here a present which I ask you to convey to him with gratitude from the Abbot and all those who worship in the Sakya-Cho Monastery."

As he spoke, he held out an envelope made of thick paper that Chandra knew was used in Tibet.

She took it from him and the Lama went on:

"Carry it to your Honourable father with our blessing, even as we bless you, our daughter, and will remember you always in our prayers."

Before Chandra could speak or thank him, the Lama said to Lord Frome:

"Guard her, my son. You have brought many treasures from our world to yours, which one day will understand their importance. In the meantime, you have found the treasure that all men seek."

"That is what I thought myself," Lord Frome said quietly.

The Lama raised his hand.

"May the Holy Buddha, the Perfect One, bless you both," he said. "Go in peace!"

After he had spoken, just as he had done before when Chandra had first met him, he closed his eyes and once again his fingers were busy with his rosary.

She knew there was nothing more to say, and, slipping her hand into Lord Frome's, they walked back towards the Bungalow.

"Will he be safe?" she asked in a low voice. "Supposing the thieves are waiting to attack him?"

"He will be safe," Lord Frome said positively. "I feel sure he will not have travelled alone, and, as you know only too well, he is protected by invisible powers."

"I am sure he is," Chandra agreed confidently, "and he told you to protect me."

"That is something I am very willing to do, and it will be easier after tomorrow."

She knew that he referred to their wedding, and as they entered the Bungalow she asked:

"Where . . . can we be . . . married?"

"I have already sent a telegram," he said, "to Patna, which is the first stop after we leave here tomorrow morning."

"I can hardly believe it!" Chandra exclaimed. "I wish I had a new gown to wear so that you will think I look beautiful."

"You will always look beautiful to me," Lord Frome said, "and as soon as we reach Delhi I intend to buy you a trousseau which will keep you happy until we can shop in London."

"You have . . . everything planned?"

"Everything!" he said positively. "And what I am really interested in, my precious one, is not what you shall wear but how soon I can hold you close in my arms—really close, without your being barred from me by those restricting quilts!"

Chandra blushed and she heard him give a little laugh.

"I am making you shy," he said, "which is something I adore doing! I shall miss that very special look in your eyes and the flood of colour in your cheeks when you become blasé about the things I say to you."

"I . . . I will . . . never do that," Chandra said, "never . . . never! And . . ."

She put her arms round his neck to whisper against his ear:

"I too will be . . . glad when there is no . . . longer any need . . . for the . . . quilts."

He pulled her closer to him and she felt his heart beating against hers.

Then his lips were on hers, fierce and passionate, so demanding that she felt as if he was a conqueror, determined to make her subservient to his demands.

It was not a shaft of sunshine that swept through

her now but the flame of fire that echoed the fire in his lips.

It seemed to rise higher and higher until it consumed them both, and far away at the back of her mind Chandra knew that this was the love which was both human and Divine.

It was somehow symbolic of Nepal itself, with its deep, warm, friendly valleys and above them the glittering, remote, snowy peaks of the unconquerable Himalayas.

This was real love, the celestial love that both men and the gods themselves sought.

"I love you, my precious darling!" she heard Lord Frome say.

Incoherently, because her happiness made it hard to speak, she managed to whisper:

"I . . . love you . . . I love you . . . there is nothing else in the . . . world . . . the sky . . . or beyond . . . but you."

ABOUT THE AUTHOR

BARBARA CARTLAND, the world's most famous romantic novelist, who is also an historian, playwright, lecturer, political speaker, and television personality, has now written over 250 books.

She has also had many historical works published and has written four autobiographies as well as the biographies of her mother and that of her brother, Ronald Cartland, who was the first Member of Parliament to be killed in the last war. This book has a preface by Sir Winston Churchill.

She has also recently completed a very unusual book called *Barbara Cartland's Book of Useless Information,* with a foreword by Admiral of the Fleet, The Earl Mountbatten of Burma. This is being sold for the United World Colleges of which he is President.

Barbara Cartland has to date sold 90 million books over the world. In 1976 she broke the world record by writing twenty-one books, and her own record in 1977 with twenty-four.

In private life Barbara Cartland, who is a Dame of the Order of St. John of Jerusalem, has fought for better conditions and salaries for midwives and nurses. As President of the Royal College of Midwives (Hertfordshire Branch) she has been invested with the first Badge of Office ever given in Great Britain, which was subscribed to by the Midwives themselves. She has also championed the cause for old people, had the law altered regarding gypsies, and founded the first Romany Gypsy Camp in the world.

Barbara Cartland is deeply interested in Vitamin Therapy and is President of the British National Association for Health. She has also sung an Album of Love Songs with the Royal Philharmonic Orchestra.